W9-CMF-073

GUIDEPOSTS

CHURCH CHOIR
MYSTERIES™

The
Un-nimble
Thimble

Roberta Updegraff

Guideposts®

CARMEL • NEW YORK 10512

www.guideposts.org

www.guideposts.org
Series Editor: Michele Slung
Cover art by Robert Tanenbaum
Cover design by Wendy Bass
Interior design by José R. Fonfrias
Interior cat illustrations by Viqui Maggio
Typeset by Composition Technologies, Inc.
Printed in the United States of America

For my darling Mark,
The man I love—husband, father and best friend.

Acknowledgments

SPECIAL APPRECIATION to my beautiful Honduran sisters, especially Deleana and Ledy. Thanks to José Rodas for answering questions and checking my Spanish. Fabiola, Maria looks just like you.

Thanks to my family for extending grace under pressure! Mark, Mark Claire, Sarah and Katie—and Luca, our Italian son. A hug to Evelyn for helping in so many little ways.

Much appreciation to Eileen M. Berger, my mentor and dear friend. Thanks to Roberta Brosius and Ellen Tinsman for editing. Love to my critique buddies in West Branch Christian Writers. And thanks to Penn Garvin Orbaker for being a special friend and reading the manuscript.

Thanks to my Guideposts Book editors, Elizabeth Kramer Gold and Michele Slung, for being so supportive. I love these characters! It is a fun project.

GRACIE REPOSITIONED HERSELF for the umpteenth time on the under-padded folding chair. Her bunions were killing her, but she couldn't very well take off her shoes to rub them—not when half the people in Willow Bend were watching.

Lord, just give me a little rest from the aching, she implored silently, pushing with the toe of one shoe against the heel of the other in order to release a dress pump from her foot.

"Aa-hhh."

"*Hmm?*" Marge Lawrence leaned into Gracie's shoulder and whispered, "You say something?"

"Bunions."

"Onions?" Marge gasped, holding her hand close to her mouth, carefully avoiding the Melon Frost lipstick Gracie had watched her meticulously apply before the choir took their places in the loft. "I have onion breath?"

Gracie smiled, accepting her best friend's obsession with her looks. The fifties had been trying years for her, too, she remembered—too young for the senior citizen fringes, but old enough so no one would lament your dying young. "No, dearie, you don't have bad breath," she whispered back. "I was referring to my *bun*ions."

Estelle Livett shot them a warning glance. Eternal Hope's diva was not only the sole member of the choir with formal voice training, but was also the self-proclaimed queen of the choir. Gracie smiled sweetly, accepting the royal reprimand, and Estelle's posture softened.

A bit of a know-it-all, that was true—but Gracie was convinced that Estelle had a softer side, too. Now if she could just figure out how to bring that softer side to the surface! On days like this, though, it seemed a daunting task.

You and me Lord, we'll just have to love *her into submission.*

Eternal Hope Community Church was a large factor in Gracie's life, and her fellow choir members were all dear friends. They'd steadfastly been there when she lost Elmo, her grief yet unfinished. And it had been almost five years since her husband died.

As if reading her mind, Marge squeezed her hand. She also knew these phantom pangs. Marge had been twice widowed, and her third husband would be dead if she could ever catch up with him! Thoughts of her feisty friend buoyed Gracie's spirits, and she returned her attention to the service.

The occasion was Willow Bend's monthly ecumenical lunch program. *Pretty good turnout. Especially since the speakers are missionaries—well, missionaries of sorts.* "Harold and Jean Meyer," she'd read in the program, "are both retired teachers who for the last year have been in Honduras helping with the cleanup of recent hurricane damage."

Gracie leaned forward to get a better look at the pair as the woman said, "Pastor Paul Meyer of Eternal Hope Community Church is our son—"

"And we're proud of him!" the man chimed in.

So are we. Gracie scanned the stage to catch Paul's eye. Her minister straightened and smiled at his parents. *Such a lovely young man. And a heart of gold to boot.* She was sad that his engagement to that girl from back East hadn't worked out, for Gracie was old-fashioned enough to believe the man needed a wife. Someone sweet, a woman who loved kids. Gracie could imagine them with a pair of tow-headed children. She had a particular soft spot for little boys, as she had never raised a girl.

She felt a tender tug for her own son. She would have to call Arlen—but after five, when the rates went down. *I have half a notion to fling frugality to the wind and call Arlen right after this program!*

She could almost hear little Elmo's raspy, "Hiya, Gramma!" If only Elmo could have seen his grandson and namesake! Gracie knew she shouldn't dote on the boy, but it was hard not to, especially with the grin that melted her heart and was just like his grandfather's.

She sighed again, and turned her attention back to the speakers. Paul looked like his father, with the same sandy-colored hair, but he had his mother's blue eyes.

Gracie wondered what Jean thought about her son's still being a bachelor. Some folks claimed to see a bohemian streak in Paul—but that didn't bother Gracie who was a little offbeat herself. She smiled. What was wrong with eccentricity, anyway? She liked quirks of all sorts.

Paul was certainly an advocate for missions.

She glanced again at the young man. Lately he'd been looking a bit glum. Could it be because he thought Eternal Hope wasn't jumping on the global outreach bandwagon as quickly as he'd hoped? She had tried to explain the congregation's reaction. It wasn't that they didn't believe in mission; why, the board had appropriated a whopping thirty percent of the budget to mission causes. Yep, they were as mission-minded as any bunch of saints. But what Paul failed to notice was that a large portion of the flock was gray-headed. Present company excluded. What was it Clairol called this shade? Tangelo Spice. Just plain red would have been fine with her, for even the sound of the word declared "yes" to life. *Red*, she shouted silently.

I'm here for You, Lord! On the ground and running. Just hold that crown a couple more decades. She shot an apologetic glance heavenward. *If that's all right with You, that is.*

Gracie felt an invisible nudge to pay attention. Jean Meyer was recounting the devastation caused by the hurricane. The tropical storm had cost thousands of lives, caused billions of dollars worth of damage and had left an already poor country devastated.

"It will probably take another ten years, at least, until Honduras is even able to recoup the marginal economic stability it had achieved before the storm," Harold was adding.

Gracie listened to his report on the economic consequences of the storm, and had to agree that it looked like the second poorest country in the Western Hemisphere was destined to remain that for a very long time.

"What can we do?" someone asked.

"Pray," came the gentle voice of Jean Meyer. "And look for places to tap into recovery efforts. Donate money—get your church to construct individual health, hygiene or school kits. Join a work team. But I want you to know," she cautioned, "that the Hondurans don't need even our financial support as much as they need our friendship. They have been through a lot. They're grieving and trying to put their lives back together. What greater gift can we give but empathy—friendship."

Harold nodded. "Offering your time and labor is a good

way to demonstrate that. Some churches are even establishing partnerships with Latino congregations, forging friendships that will become reciprocal as the people in Honduras get back on their feet."

"Speaking of which," Jean interjected, "we want to introduce the newest member of our family." She beckoned to the podium a tan little girl with a shy smile. "This is Maria, our daughter."

Grinning brightly, Maria looked up adoringly at her. Jean hugged her, saying, "Maria lost her family in the mudslide caused by the hurricane. She was one of the few survivors in her *barrio*."

"This little girl has been through a lot." Harold rubbed the girl's back. "But she has *Doña* Coca," he said, motioning at the well-worn doll the child held.

He said something tender in Spanish, and the girl caressed the doll while replying in perfect English. "God sent *Don* Harold and *Doña* Jean to take care of us. For this I am very grateful."

"And so are we!" Jean exclaimed.

Gracie couldn't help but feel warmed by this display of affection.

"*El Diablo*—that hurricane," Maria said softly, bottom lip trembling. "He took *every*thing. It was very hard for me to understand why this should happen to us. Only now can I trust El Señor because He took care of me."

Jean put her arm around Maria and rubbed her small straight back. "It's okay, dear, you don't have to say anything more. The people understand that it is hard to talk about."

Maria shook her head, continuing. "The storm came and the houses began to slide into the water. We were all running. I fell and thought that I am dead. I felt arms lift me. I thought it was an angel, but Pastor Reyes took me to his church— *Iglesia de Esperanza.*"

"Church of Hope," Jean translated.

"There were many children at his church. Many without fathers or mothers. So many I did not hope to find my mamma. They told me not to lose hope—but I knew hope was only for those with family. I was alone. I thought I had no one to help me."

Maria paused, seeming to give time for the solemnity of her situation to sink in. Jean's hand again caressed Maria's back as the child continued her story. "It was then that I lost all hope. I wanted to die myself, and begged God to take me, too." She searched the audience with her steady gaze, then looked straight at Gracie. "But He did not.

"I felt the angels again—all around me. The saints of *Iglesia de Esperanza*—they carried me through that dark time."

"These beautiful people," Harold interjected. "They kept the faith for each other. They carried each other."

It was at that moment Gracie understood—*knew*—there was to be a special bond between her and this young person.

13

And between her and Paul's parents. But what that something special was, God had yet to inform her.

Now, Gracie listened even more closely as Jean and Harold went on to explain the dream they had for that Honduran church. It was a shared dream, which envisioned a sewing cooperative that could create handicrafts to be sold through an ecumenical service organization, one that would act as distributor for other entrepreneurial endeavors in Third World countries. The dream also included the construction of an addition to the church, providing space for a preschool and day care center.

Gracie was impressed with the depth of commitment these survivors had made to one another. Only a few of the twenty families from the same neighborhood who'd sought shelter in the *Iglesia de Esperanza* during the storm had been members, and they'd brought the others. Many, like Maria, had lost everything, but they had found an abundance of encouragement and hope there.

They'd organized themselves with a list of priorities, making the most vulnerable—the single mothers with children— their first priority for new houses. Mr. and Mrs. Meyer had been among those making up the construction crew for the first three homes, and their denomination had supplied funds for the project.

The reception following the program was fine—for what it was. Still, Gracie couldn't help comparing the food with what she would have provided had she and Marge catered the event. The broccoli soup, for example, was good, considering it was made with milk instead of cream (and she did admit that milk was better for a person's health). But couldn't they have done better than plain cake for dessert?

She was just about to finish her slice when she saw Jean Meyer across the table. "Wonderful presentation," Gracie told the woman as she introduced herself. "I was really moved by what you had to say." Gracie moved closer. "I'm going to talk to the choir about organizing something to do to help."

Jean nodded, smiling politely, as she scanned the area to check on Maria, who was enjoying her dessert at a nearby table.

"I also wanted to say how sorry I am to hear of the child's loss."

Jean again only nodded, causing Gracie just for an instant to regret her pull toward the little girl and the couple who were caring for her. "I'm sorry—Mrs. . . ?"

"Parks. Gracie Parks."

The woman explained, "I'm a bit overprotective. It's been a long time since we've had a child in the house. Paul was an only child—until Maria."

"I can certainly understand. My Arlen is an only child. I still fuss over him, and he's got a wife and a boy of his own!"

Jean seemed to relax. "I thought it was a grandchild I'd be spoiling, but Paul seems in no hurry to find a wife. I was disappointed that his engagement didn't work out. Paul's got a head on his shoulders, so I trust he made the right decision."

"Now he has become the most eligible bachelor in the church." Gracie couldn't believe she was sharing this! "Why, I know several women with nieces, friends and acquaintances—all sweet girls, girls they think would be just right for Pastor Paul."

Jean chuckled. "It's just getting him to notice. His career is everything. Serving the Lord, he tells me. I tell him a wife is a partner. That's two servants for the price of one."

Jean glanced at Maria again, who was now chatting with a girl about the same age.

"Suzy Hadlock. Nice girl. A neighbor of mine."

Jean sighed. "You probably think I'm paranoid, but someone's just telephoned my son's house, asking about us and whether we had adopted a Honduran girl. Asked Paul a lot of questions. Nothing important—just how long Harold and I were staying. The man said he was a freelance writer looking for story possibilities, but I wish I knew. You hear so much in the news. And Maria loves the computer. She's been using it a lot at Paul's house. We keep it monitored, but I worry all the same." She gave a nervous laugh. "I'm too old to be a parent!"

Gracie touched Jean's arm. "I admire you greatly."

They stood in companionable silence, until Marge blasted

her with, "Gracie Parks, I saw you take that extra slice of cake!"

Stopping just short of running into her, Marge hooked her hand on her hip and fixed Gracie with that Jimminy Cricket stare of hers. "You're watching your weight, hon, remember?"

Gracie felt herself flush, realizing she was still holding the second plate.

"Now I'll just toss that thing in the garbage—for both our sakes."

That familiar twinkle made Gracie smile. Marge did sincerely care for her well-being, she knew. Gracie couldn't help but laugh. "You saved me!"

Marge let out a dramatic sigh of relief, then pivoted to face Jean. "We've just got to do something for you, honey. Your daughter's story put me in tears. I just wanted to reach out and hug you all." With that, Marge embraced the woman, giving her a fierce hug.

"I'm thinking we could maybe make those health-care kits I keep reading about. My head is just bubbling with ideas. Why, I'm practically a one-woman fountain of good will!"

Gracie touched her friend's shoulder. "Take a breath, relax, Marge. Let's have proper introductions first. Jean Meyer, this is Marge Lawrence, my dearest friend. She owns a gift shop and often helps when I cater."

Marge surveyed her from head to toe. "Thank goodness

you traded those *awful* sneakers of yours for a pair of pumps. She has the kind that have the little light in the sole-cushion, the kind the kids wear."

Gracie was about to defend herself when Marge put her hand up, stop-fashion. "Don't even mention your bunions! Respectable ladies do not have *bunions*!"

Apparently satisfied that she'd set Gracie on the path to sophistication and charm, Marge turned her attention to Jean. "Now, how long are you going to be in the States, and in Willow Bend?"

"About six months. We're staying with Paul. We want to enroll Maria in school, and speak to churches in the area, where I hope to get support for the cooperative. We would like to get the sewing cooperative working as soon as possible."

"How wonderful. We'll look forward to your getting involved with the women's group, maybe even the choir. You can sing, can't you? Well never mind if you can't, we love listeners equally."

"Of course." Jean laughed and so did Gracie.

Then Jean told Marge, "I look forward to getting involved in Paul's community. But give us a couple of weeks to settle in, please."

"Certainly." Marge seemed delighted with her new friend. "Now we just need a project—something special to promote interest in Honduras."

Gracie thought of the *Guideposts* story about a Romanian orphan who, after being adopted and growing up in the United States, had become an advocate for street children in her native country by starting a sewing circle in her church to provide blankets for orphans. "Blankets! That's it!"

She looked at Marge. "We could make 'blankies'—security blankets. Or teddy bears. Special gifts for the children in the shelter. What do you think?"

"Sounds like a good idea." Jean seemed genuinely excited.

"Blankets sound easier than teddy bears," Marge interjected. "And we used to have a sewing circle. We could get that going again. I love to crochet, even though I haven't done anything in years."

"Blankets it is!"

Jean looked back at Maria. Gracie felt a nudge. *Lord, what is it? What would You would have me see, to understand about this child?*

19

I T'S A NEW RECIPE." Gracie slid the plate in front of
Uncle Miltie. She wanted to be patient, but her darling
relative was tweaking her last nerve. It wasn't like him to be
so cantankerous. George Morgan, always known as Miltie,
was a good man, and always trying to be helpful. She understood how grateful he was to her for sharing her home with
him after his wife had died.

She should have known not to spring something new on
him, especially after serving him that disaster of a Mexican
dish a few nights before. Gracie made a mental note to talk to
Jean Meyer about Honduran cuisine. It would give them
common ground for developing a friendship, and, besides,
Gracie had been hankering for some mildly spicy food.

Of course, Uncle Miltie would be a tough sell on trying a

spicy dish again, after almost singeing his nostrils with chili peppers. Besides, the old man stuck like epoxy to the past. He reveled in the familiar. She grinned, thinking Uncle Miltie considered Spam gourmet fare.

"Look at dinnertime as an adventure," she told him, returning to the counter to get the next dish. "Didn't you say that you always wanted to go to Greece? Well, tonight, we're eating Mediterranean."

"I know, I know, you found a really great cookbook."

"Why, yes, I did!"

"How many of them can there be out there, anyway? You must own them all by now."

Gracie shook her head, trying to retain her good mood. "Your sacroiliac acting up again?"

"Same old nuisance pain." He relaxed a little. "That noticeable, huh?"

She bent to kiss his head. "Take your pain medicine. I know you don't like prescriptions. You're a tough old bird, but there's no sense in suffering. Especially when you've got something to relieve the pain. And, Uncle dear, it is just strong aspirin—nothing addictive."

"I've heard of folks getting addicted to aspirin." He shook a finger at her. "A person can't be too careful, you know. They tamper with things. Folks have died from aspirin. And people do get addicted to things as mild as aspirin, Gracie."

She exhaled frustration, giving his shoulder a pat. "I guess a person can become addicted to almost anything. But they make the bottles tamper-proof now, so take the pills, Uncle Miltie, for both our sakes."

"All right, all right!" He put his hand up, stop-fashion. "But not until after supper. Not on an empty stomach."

He was cantankerous, but lovable. "Your stomach is never empty," she reminded him. "I saw the scoop missing in the peach-a-berry cobbler. Someone's been sampling—and it wasn't Gooseberry!"

"You're certain, eh?" Miltie feigned innocence. "That cat's got weird tastes. He's spiteful enough to try and frame me."

Uncle Miltie and the cat were having a battle of sorts. Gooseberry considered himself the alpha male of their household, and was not about to yield an inch to another, even one of the human variety. For his part, Uncle Miltie was not inclined to give the feline a speck of satisfaction, unless he was feeling magnanimous.

She chuckled inside. *My boys!*

Uncle Miltie spooned some of the tomato-and-parsley dish into Gracie's salad bowl and then his. "What's this stuff? Land sakes, girl, can't we just have meat and potatoes?"

"It is tabouli."

"*Bo-looey!* Give me good ol' tossed salad with *dee*licious Thousand Island dressing! Save this gunk for the high-falutin' folks who hire you to cater their fancy dinner parties. What else are we having?"

"A nice roast ... Mediterranean style."

A harumph.

Gracie knew he'd eat it. "The man likes to hear himself complain," Aunt Doris used to say, "but when it comes to food he's a steam shovel!" Gracie smiled, remembering him complimenting his wife on the very meal he would have grumbled about to her *before* he ate it.

"It's done with dried tomatoes," Gracie told him. "And Kalamata olives."

"Kala-whata?"

"Olives. You like *olives*, don't you?"

"I guess. I'll eat anything you fix." His grumble was half-hearted. Then he looked at her and smiled. "I love you, Gracie. You've been good to me. I hate being such a bother. Just out of sorts, I guess."

She plunked two pills in front of his glass of water. "You need the help of a little pharmacology! Don't you argue with me, George Morgan!"

"Now you sound like Doris!" He swallowed the pills with a swig of water. "Satisfied?"

Gracie patted his head. "Satisfied." She put the rest of the meal on the table.

"I'm darn near starved."

Gracie rolled her eyes.

"I'm still a growing boy."

This time she laughed. "You're a long way past that."

"Isn't that the truth!"

She was pulling out her chair when she remembered, "I forgot the butter!"

Reaching for the door she heard, "Wait!" and turned to Uncle Miltie.

"You don't want to catch the salad *dressing*, now do you?"

Uncle Miltie gave a guffaw. She couldn't help but let herself laugh with him. Her uncle never tired of his corny jokes, most of them ancient and the rest hardly fresh, but always managed to get a chuckle. Gracie figured it was his infectious, self-appreciative laugh, more than his skill as a comedian, that worked on his audience, even including her.

After sitting down at the table, Gracie bowed her head and waited for Uncle Miltie to do the same. He smiled, acknowledging their nightly tradition. "Lord, thank You for this food," he began, "and the hands that prepared it."

Gracie had a lot on her mind and couldn't resist interrupting their usual routine. "We are incredibly blessed, Father God. We take too much for granted, especially me. Forgive me for that. Help me to be appreciative of all our blessings . . ."

She felt Uncle Miltie's confused stare, but kept her head bowed. "We remember the Hondurans and their struggle just to put bread on the table. . . ." Gracie felt her throat tighten, recalling Maria's story and the situation in Honduras.

"Bless this food," Uncle Miltie began again after her interjection, "and us to your service. In Jesus' name we pray."

"Amen." Gracie finished, feeling affection for his familiar before-meal words. Silently, she once again thanked God for bringing the two of them together.

Uncle Miltie reached for the mashed potatoes. "Now, this is American cuisine!"

"I did them Mediterranean style according to the cookbook." Gracie sat back and watched him spoon the food onto his dish. She loved taking care of people. She loved homemaking, especially the part that included the offering of food to others. El had been fond of saying that she'd dazzled him so with her home-cooking that he had had no choice but to propose. How that man loved to eat! And he'd displayed a waistline that hinted strongly of his passion. Gracie used to pat it with pride.

Lord, how I miss that man!

"Mashed potatoes," Miltie reiterated, "Can't get more American than that. If the Greeks want to eat them, it's okay by me. I am thankful they eat something I recognize."

This man was a delight also. Now she marked life "before" and "after" Uncle Miltie. Before he came to live with her, life hadn't seemed half so interesting. She'd been mourning Elmo's death in a way that was plainly not healthy. It was after Doris died that she realized she'd been pining over the past. Living with memories. Not moving on. El never would have wanted that. They'd promised each other to go on, to live life to the fullest even without the other.

Yes, Uncle Miltie's coming to live with her had been a godsend—for both of them. They'd been good for each other. Miltie Morgan was the independent sort, but he had adored his wife of fifty-six years, of that Gracie was certain.

Aunt Doris had been easy to love, with a radar for folks who needed a hug or a pan of her famous apple betty. Her dying of cancer had been a hard blow for all of them, that was true. But the woman had known her place in the world: she was a child of God, to be sure, one whom the Lord had taken home just a few months short of her eightieth birthday.

She'd been a brave woman, too. Her eyes, even though dulled by pain, had kept their sparkle. She remained the encourager right up until the end.

Oh, Lord, to live my dying days with such dignity!

She reached for Uncle Miltie's hand. "I'm thankful for your friendship."

Uncle Miltie feigned a scowl. "You're not going soft on me, are you, Gracie girl? You know, I hate that sentimental stuff." His gaze met hers. "You're thinking about your Aunt Doris, aren't you?"

"Just missing her a little."

"There isn't a day goes by I don't think about that woman." This time he squeezed her hand. "She was purely something. Purely special."

They sat in companionable silence for a couple of minutes.

Uncle Miltie took another bite of potatoes. "After dinner I'm going to fix that electrical receptacle on the back porch." He glanced her way for confirmation. "Think there's a short in the wiring. We don't want a fire."

"What would I do without you?"

He put a palm up. "A man's got to earn his keep."

She smiled and refilled their glasses with water.

"Truth be known," he said, "I'm probably more bother than I'm worth. I just appreciate your taking me in."

"Taking you in? You were the life-saver! Why, I probably would have fallen and broken my hip on that creaky old back porch step, had you not replaced it. And the bookshelves in the study are nice as any craftsman could make. . . .

"In short, you're a gem, Uncle Miltie. How could I part with you?"

He dismissed that with a wave of hand between bites.

"Don't you go flirting with any available widows!" she teased. "Do you hear me? I have a lot of projects that still need doing."

He chuckled, but his expression told her that he was touched by her response.

"So, why all this sudden interest in Honduras?"

Uncle Miltie leaned back in his chair as Gracie filled him in on the luncheon and all that the Meyers had shared. She was telling him about Marge's ideas for helping when there was a knock at the back door.

"Is that your fine coffee I smell?" Rocky Gravino inquired, taking a big whiff. "What will it cost a guy to get a cup?"

Gracie stood to get the pot. "I was just going to fix us some peach-a-berry cobbler. You want some?"

"I can't say no to any cobbler, ever, that's for sure." Rocky pulled out a chair next to Uncle Miltie and made small talk while Gracie fixed three plates of dessert.

Rocky was a handsome man whose salt-and-pepper hair— a bit longish for a sixty-nine-year-old—enhanced his look of distinction. "Brawny," was how Marge described Willow Bend's newspaper editor and Gracie couldn't help but agree.

Marge actually had decided Rocky was smitten with Gracie, and her teasing about it was almost enough to drive her friend mad. But Gracie adored her next-door neighbor: Marge Lawrence was just about the best ally and pal a woman could ask for.

Rocky was a good friend, too. He and Elmo had hit it off from almost the first minute Rocky arrived in town from Philadelphia. He had been her husband's dear companion, and sounding board, even when they disagreed, and it was natural that he'd appoint himself her guard dog. These last few years, he had gradually become one of her closest confidants. But there was nothing romantic between them, as she had constantly to remind Marge.

Gracie sensed Rocky had come for more than dessert. She sat the plate in front of him and sat down again. "So what's up?"

A knowing grin. "You can read me like a newspaper."

"Can't hide nothing from Gracie," Miltie said, digging into his bowl of warm cobbler. "My oh my, mighty fine! I'd say darn near as tasty as Doris's apple betty."

Gracie made a mental note to hunt for her aunt's recipe.

"Spent the afternoon fishing with Herb," Rocky began. "Didn't catch a thing, but got a lead on a story. And the *Mason County Gazette* sure could use a headliner."

"Herb got a dispatch—Pastor Paul's house was broken into. They weren't sure when, though, since the family had been out of town overnight. He and his parents were at a speaking engagement in Avery. They stayed over with the pastor and his wife."

Uncle Miltie started in surprise, pulling himself erect. "More shenanigans in Willow Bend!"

"Let's not jump to conclusions," Gracie interjected. "Are they sure it was robbery?"

Rocky shrugged. "Don't know much yet. Herb is with Paul right now. I wanted to go along, but Herb didn't think it was a good idea. Mrs. Meyer is pretty upset, and he was afraid a newspaperman might make her more nervous."

"But you're their friend, Rocky." Gracie tried to sound encouraging. "Paul probably would have liked the moral support."

Rocky took a sip of coffee. "Mmmm, your brew is the best, Gracie." He paused to savor it. "You might be right about

Paul not minding, but this is police business. I respect Herb's judgment.

"Must admit, I would like a story, though." He took another sip.

"*Hmmph!*" Uncle Miltie sniffed. "This is the Midwest! We're just *folks!* Willow Bend is our piece of heaven this side of eternity. Robberies aren't included in the celestial description!" He nodded snappily for emphasis. "Why, three-quarters of the folks in town don't even lock their back doors!"

"Like I said," Rocky went on, "I don't know much. Herb dropped me off here on the way to the pastor's place. I did hear him talking to Paul on the phone, though. Paul said nothing is missing. There wasn't even a window broken because he'd left the back door *unlocked.*"

"What did I tell you?" Uncle Miltie said.

Gracie was perplexed. "So how did he know the place was broken into if nothing was missing?"

Rocky scratched his chin. "Don't rightly know. I guess there was a mess. Somebody went through the dresser drawers, I think Herb said."

"So what exactly *do* they know, Rocky?" Gracie asked.

"Nothing for sure. I was having coffee with Herb when the call came in. I wanted to go along, but he was going to pick up Jim Thompson. They didn't seem open to having a reporter trail along. Personally, Jim's a good guy, one of the best, but he just doesn't have a nose for investigation. I thought I'd go over there and snoop around, and take you with me. You have that sixth sense, Gracie."

Gracie was mulling over the facts, but her sympathy was with Paul. Such an invasion of privacy! She couldn't imagine discovering someone had been through her things. What if they discovered that slinky negligee Elmo had given her years ago? Never mind that it was probably two sizes too small, she just couldn't bear to part with it. She refocused on the situation. "I'd guess the family is pretty shook up."

Rocky nodded. "Figured as much. I told Herb I'd pop in on you, maybe wait here for a call saying it was all right to call on the Meyers. Besides, I knew you'd be serving dessert about this time, and Gracie, you *are* the finest cook in town!"

"Mighty fine," Uncle Miltie concurred, wiping the crumbs off his shirt front. "She makes the best flaky pastry in the entire county, maybe even the whole state."

"But what about my tabouli?"

He grinned. "Tab—ooley is fine, too."

"Yep, you're the best, Gracie!" Rocky seconded.

Gracie felt herself blush. Then, remembering the situation, she asked, "What about the family? Paul's parents? Poor Maria—she's been through so much already."

Uncle Miltie glanced at his niece. "The little girl?"

"Thankfully," Rocky said, "Maria was with them. They were all out of town together. At least that's what Herb said. I'm going to call him in a little while—get more information."

31

"Do you have any idea who might have done it?" Gracie found herself lost for motives. Paul was probably one of the most respected people in town. Besides, he didn't own much of anything and maintained a simple lifestyle, claiming it was a hangover from his divinity school days.

"Not a clue," Rocky told her. "It just doesn't make sense. Especially since nothing was taken. They left the stereo and laptop computer."

Gracie shook her head. "There's got to be more to it."

"That's what I figure," Rocky said, propping his elbows on the table and resting his chin on his knuckles. "I thought you were just the person to ask. Why, Gracie, you know just about everything about everybody."

She felt herself blush again. "Well, I don't know about that."

"Well of course you do," Uncle Miltie confirmed. "You're a natural listener. Some folks would use that knack to gossip, but not you, Gracie. You care. Folks sense that."

Her "thank you" was meek but heartfelt.

"I'd like to question the pastor. Ask him whether he might have made someone mad enough to seek revenge."

"Revenge?" Gracie cringed. This was getting out of hand. Pastor Paul was the sweetest man—wouldn't hurt a fly! Why, she'd seen him usher spiders to the outdoors, rather than kill them in his house. Who could hold a grudge against Paul?

"Burglars don't usually rob friends," Uncle Miltie pointed out. "We're all friends here in Willow Bend. I tend to agree with Rocky. There's got to be more to it."

"Like I said," Rocky reiterated, "I don't know much of anything yet. We're all in the waiting stage."

"You're sure nothing was taken?" Gracie asked.

"Somebody could have scared the burglars, so they didn't have time to steal anything," Rocky replied.

"We do have a neighborhood watch," Uncle Miltie pointed out. "Anyone check with them?"

Rocky was obviously considering the possibilities. "Thought I'd give Herb time to sort things out." He looked at Gracie. "In the meantime, I figured I'd drop over and get a chance to hear what you think."

"Too much Agatha Christie," Uncle Miltie teased. "She keeps the library in business."

"Gracie does have a flair for mystery." Rocky's expression was amiable.

"She likes untangling knots, too," Uncle Miltie added.

Gracie made a mock bow.

"Seriously, Gracie, how about casually dropping in at Pastor Paul's. Poke around a bit and ask a few questions? Can't hurt."

Uncle Miltie cleared his throat. "If you ask me, and you didn't, but then, I never was one to keep my opinion to myself. Perhaps it was kids—kids being mischievous. After all, you said Paul reported nothing was missing. Some drawers were gone through, so perhaps they just wanted to get something on the pastor."

"That's a good point," Rocky conceded, glancing at Gracie. "What do you say we check it out?"

Gracie nodded, thinking that Paul and his family might welcome the support. "Another scoop of cobbler?"

He patted his stomach. "I don't want to loose my girlish figure."

Uncle Miltie let out a big, juicy burst of laughter. "Girlish figure! You got a good case of Dunlap's disease. Your waist *done lapped* over your belt, man!"

Rocky snorted.

"Boys!"

Uncle Miltie reached for his walker. "If you're going to the scene of the crime, I'm going with you. Might be some fixing needing done after all that commotion, and I'm just the man to do it."

PAUL LIVED HALFWAY BETWEEN Gracie's place and the church. He'd bought a 1920s-style stucco, a "fixer-upper," it was called. It was a nice-sized house, though, with three bedrooms. Paul had said he always wanted his own place, and rentals were hard to find in Willow Bend. He'd bought it a couple of weeks after starting at the church. It hardly seemed three years ago. Paul was excited now to be able to host his parents, who'd sold their home to make themselves available for mission.

The plaster was worn, and green paint was peeling off the window frames, but the dwelling did have charm. Paul had done a lot to the inside. The church had thrown a painting party to lend a hand. Gracie herself had helped to wax and polish the lovely oak woodwork.

She was glad his parents would be living with Paul for a few months. Even with all the help the church folks were willing to give, the place still needed much more done. Harold Meyer was robust, the handy type, Gracie knew. Paul, bless his heart, was all thumbs when it came to carpentry. She laughed, remembering Uncle Miltie claiming, "The pastor cut the board three times and still couldn't figure out why it was too short."

Gracie eased her dignified Cadillac, Fannie Mae, behind Herb's cruiser. The engine coughed when she turned off the key. "Poor baby, we've got to get you into Harry's garage for a checkup."

She glanced at Rocky sitting beside her. "I have her oil changed every two thousand miles, like clockwork. El would be proud of me."

"Sure would." Rocky gave her shoulder a quick pat. "You've come a long way, Gracie. I remember him saying you wouldn't even pump gas. If I recall correctly you used to think that the letter *E* on the gauge stood for *Enough*. That meant it was *enough* to get you home, and so El always got stuck with putting gas in the old girl."

She laughed. "I still don't pump if I can get out of it."

"Say, look!" Uncle Miltie poked her from the back seat. "Isn't that Marge's car in the driveway?"

"Well," Rocky said. "So it is. That woman has better news sense than most of my reporters."

Paul invited them in, where Marge had coffee ready. She bade them take a seat at the kitchen table, with that give-me-a-minute wink of hers. Gracie gathered from what they were talking about that Marge had been there a while. By this time Harold and Jean Meyer were sitting at the table. Herb was leaning against the counter sipping coffee. All present must have tired of second-guessing the case, for they now sat around the table, making small talk.

Gracie opened and placed on the table a plastic container of chocolate chip cookies which she had retrieved from her freezer just before leaving. Uncle Miltie was talking to Paul, but on hearing the snap of a plastic lid, he ambled over and reached for a handful of cookies. Before she could scold Uncle Miltie, Paul also grabbed a few. She could only smile, wishing she'd brought another container.

"I love your cookies, Gracie. Mom's not much for baking."

"Hey, hey, hey! That's my wife you're talking about."

Paul flashed his father a sheepish grin. "Sorry, I didn't think I said anything that wasn't common knowledge."

"It's fine, dear." Jean patted his hand. "I never was much of a baker. Lucky for me, you loved Oreos and Fig Newtons."

"Yes, I do remember." Harold chuckled, turning toward his son. "Paul loved those cookies. But your mother *has* learned to cook, I want you to know. She and Armando make a mean tortilla!"

He explained to the rest of them, "Armando was our cook. He works at the Christian retreat center where we stayed while in Honduras."

"I began by carrying dishes out to the kitchen," Jean told them. "A few compliments later we were chopping vegetables for avocado *ensalada*. The rest is culinary history."

Harold looked at his wife with fondness. "Your mother is fast mastering a new cuisine."

Marge put cups and saucers in front of Gracie, Uncle Miltie and Rocky. Herb took a seat at the table. "Save a few of those cookies for me," he reminded Uncle Miltie.

"Got some sugar for the coffee, Margie?" Uncle Miltie teased.

"I haven't been Margie since...." Marge stood with coffee pot in hand, overdramatizing her pondering. "Well, since high school anyway, and that's too long ago to remember."

"Why you don't look a day older than... ah, *thirty*." Uncle Miltie chuckled.

Gracie swatted Uncle Miltie gently on the back. "Flattery will get you nowhere with Marge. She's on to you. So watch yourself!"

Gracie seized the moment to get to know Jean better. "Do you think you could teach me to make Armando's *ensalada*? I've been meaning to try my hand at Mexican cuisine."

Uncle Miltie cleared his throat. "What about that chili you made the other night? Darn near singed my taste buds!"

"That's why I need some help," Gracie laughed, going with the fun. She *had* overseasoned it, putting chili pepper in twice. A call from Barb Jennings had distracted her. That woman fussed more over the choir than most mothers do their newborns.

"The chili didn't set right on my delicate stomach," Uncle Miltie explained, garnering all the sympathy he could.

"Delicate stomach, my derriere, George Morgan!" Marge rolled her eyes. "I've seen you at the church pot-luck dinners! That man can out-eat a horse," she told Jean.

"I do recall," Gracie gently reminded him, "you ate three helpings of that chili before topping it with chocolate ice cream."

Uncle Miltie grimaced. "Now that you mention it, it probably was the ice cream."

Everyone laughed.

"You must have a stainless steel stomach," Rocky said.

"I really couldn't sleep," he said, still trying to acquire sympathy. "I was up half the night."

"Why doesn't that surprise me? Chili and chocolate ice cream. What did you expect—sweet and spicy dreams?" Marge was having fun.

Gracie came to his defense. "He did have a bad night. A lot of foods are not agreeing with him. I do need to be a bit more careful." She couldn't resist the reprimand. "But the man resists taking any medication—not even antacid."

"Stubborn old coot!" Rocky said. "That's how he is with

everything. Don't even think of turning the chess board. He likes it just off center."

"Watch who you're calling a coot!" Uncle Miltie wagged a finger. "And who always wins, Gravino, huh? You win the game—you turn the board to suit yourself."

"'Curmudgeonly' sounds more dignified," Gracie offered. Another round of laughter.

Gracie enjoyed these people, and hoped Paul's parents would come to love them, too. She smiled at Jean. "We tease Uncle Miltie, but actually he's a great guy. He keeps active doing volunteer work—visits at the senior center and reads to the kids at the elementary school. He does odd jobs, too."

"Not to mention he's a bit odd himself," Rocky added, smiling. "But I guess he's entitled to be, at his age."

"Watch who you're calling old!" Uncle Miltie thumped his chest. "There's more than a few years left in me. Got me a new lease on life—a regulator for the tick-tocker."

"A pacemaker doesn't make you invincible," Marge reminded him. "You've got to eat right, and get exercise."

"Don't you worry about me," he told her. "I'm going *wear* out before I *rust* out!"

Gracie patted his hand again. "We should all do so well at your age."

"My age?" He straightened. "Why, what have I been telling you, girlie. Age is just a state of mind."

"That it is," she agreed.

Jean held up a cookie. "These are good. Just like my mother used to make. I'd love the recipe."

"Old family recipe," Gracie confessed, tongue in cheek. "Right off the back of the chip bag—a forty-year-old bag, that is."

Jean's curiosity was piqued, so Gracie explained: "As a girl, I used to spend summers with Uncle Miltie and Aunt Doris. On rainy days, we'd bake together. She used the recipe on the package, so I figured what was good enough for her was good enough for me. Took an empty bag home and have been using it ever since."

Jim Thompson appeared in the doorway. "Talked to the neighbors—no one saw anything. The woman next door didn't hear anything either. The old girl admits to using a hearing aid. Didn't have it in, of course."

His gaze narrowed to Paul. "And it doesn't help that you left the back door unlocked."

"I meant to lock it, really, I did. Just forgot."

Marge defended him. "I've done the same lots of times."

"I think we all have," Gracie admitted.

Herb stroked his chin. "Any other leads?"

"Got the folks in the graveyard behind the park, but don't think they're talking, chief." Jim laughed at his own attempt to be funny.

Uncle Miltie snorted appreciatively.

Herb ignored the jest. "You talk to the regulars over at the park? Joggers, folks walking their dogs, parents with kids? See if someone noticed anything coming or going from there?"

Jim shook his head. "Too late today. I'll do that first thing tomorrow morning, though."

"It could have been the *kids*," Marge interjected. "A bunch of teenagers hang out in that park. They were pretty miffed about Paul banning skateboards in the church parking lot. Maybe they were trying to get even."

Rocky nodded. "Makes sense, Marge. A couple of those teens act weirder even than Chuckie Moon used to, and that's saying a lot. I saw one boy with pierced eyebrows and a spiked collar around his neck."

"You talk to any of those kids?" Herb wanted to know.

Jim shook his head. "The park was practically deserted. Ran into Louise McCall picking the seed pods off the marigolds. She mentioned teenagers spitting on the sidewalk. Reminded me that we have a law against it on the books. She wanted me to arrest them."

"So are you going to arrest them?" Marge wanted to know. "This is a quiet town, and those boys have been up to no good before. Imagine ransacking a pastor's house. Terrible, just terrible. *Sounds* like teenagers to me."

Gracie glanced at Rocky, who had his eyes on her. *He doesn't think it was the kids, either.* They were basically good boys, even Chuckie in his green-hair stage. Their strange habits and dress unnerved folks, she had to admit, but they all came from good families. Willow Bend families. And, she reasoned, teenagers were more likely to vandalize than burglarize. "Herb, what exactly was disturbed?"

"Well as far as we can tell, Mrs. Parks," Jim interjected, "someone discovered the back door open and roamed around the house. Just nosy, I figure. Fits the 'teenagers' scenario."

Jean became a bit indignant. "They didn't just roam through our house. Our dresser drawers were rifled through. Someone went through Maria's things."

"But nothing was taken," Herb reiterated. "You said so yourself. You checked."

Harold nodded. "Nothing was taken, as far as we can tell."

"Then maybe we're on the right track," Rocky offered.

"That's right," Herb said.

Paul nodded. "I'd rather believe in opportunistic indulging of curiosity than entertain the thought of someone trying to rob or vandalize."

Herb agreed.

"You can't figure with teens," Jim said, seeming genuinely contemplative. "They're unpredictable. Look at their hair— green one day, red the next. Those boys were pretty upset when the pastor here called me to read them the riot act."

Paul cleared his throat. "I wouldn't call it the *riot* act. They had repeatedly ignored my ban on riding those boards in the church parking lot. I suggested they join our youth fellowship and maybe we could work something out—get the town to construct a half-pipe, or designate a place they could officially skate. I pointed out that a parking lot simply was not a safe place. And that we were not going to tolerate smoking, spitting, and bad language on the premises." Paul paused to clarify. "Louise was the one who wanted the spitting prohibition included."

Jim nodded. "She sure is on a crusade for *that* one."

"Louise's concern aside," Herb went on, "we've still got a case to solve. I don't like the idea of snooping, either. I promised your little girl I'd get to the bottom of this."

Gracie's interested was piqued. "Maria? Poor child, she must be scared."

"Actually, it's Doña Coca, her doll, who was frightened," Harold corrected. "Maria is one tough cookie. She seemed to take it all in stride. Now she's in Paul's study, using his computer."

"Maria doesn't usually let her emotions show," Jean explained. "Doña Coca is more than security to the child, she's Maria's best friend. And Harold is right, Maria didn't act frightened. But she was the first one to realize somebody had been in the house."

"She called Jean upstairs," Harold added. "At first we thought she had merely forgotten to shut her drawers. But she's a neat child, and she insisted she'd closed them. Jean nodded. "Then we checked our room, and were sure. Clothes were hanging out of the drawers. I grabbed Maria and screamed. Paul searched the house and Harold called the police. Maria thought it was all a game, like *The Three Bears*."

"If only it *was* Goldilocks," Paul said. "The whole thing is unnerving. I agree with Herb—answers would make us feel safer."

Jean hugged herself. "It's a scary thing to know your things have been gone through."

"Poor dear." Gracie reached to squeeze her new friend's hand.

Herb wrote a few notes on his pad. "You folks try to get back to normal. We'll do what we can to get to the bottom of this."

"Should we set up surveillance, chief?" Jim asked. "I've got my car. I can take the first shift."

Herb shook his head. "No need to go to extremes."

"They could have been just casing the place," Jim defended his idea, "looking to see what they could take."

Herb shook his head. "Let's not jump to conclusions and scare these good folks."

Paul glanced between his parents. "We'll be fine. If we think of something we'll call. After all, this is Willow Bend, not Chicago. We're not going to have any more trouble."

"I'm going to head home," Marge said, putting her cup into the dishwasher. "I was on my way when I saw the police cruiser. Poor Charlotte's been penned up in the house all day, she's probably beside herself."

Marge adored her shih-tzu. Gooseberry and Charlotte had become like children.

"Did you drive, Gracie?" Marge wanted to know.

Rocky answered. "We came in Fannie Mae. I'd been with Herb, fishing, so he dropped me off at Gracie's. When we got here and saw your car in the driveway, I wondered how you'd managed to scoop Gracie."

Marge looked at her friend. "I think he's implying we're busybodies."

"Not at all," Rocky defended. "You are Willow Bend's prettiest sleuths. Where you find one, you find the other. Gracie is just usually the first one at the scene."

Marge smiled coquettishly. "Why thank you, kind sir. I like a gentleman who appreciates mature beauty."

Gracie just laughed.

4

JEAN ROLLED THE AVOCADO in her hands. "It needs to be firm but soft at the same time. They pick these things before they're ripe to ship them to the United States, so it's hard to get one that is just right. In Honduras we picked them off the trees, rich and creamy—perfect for tomato *ensalada*."

"I must admit, I seldom buy avocados." Gracie paused from dicing the tomatoes. "Don't know how to fix them. The only way I've eaten them is in guacamole, and that only once or twice."

She glanced at Jean, enjoying the camaraderie of working together. After they'd navigated what amounted to a utensil shortage, Gracie and Jean had made a list of the "essentials" needed to run a proper kitchen. They made a date for later in the week to get Paul properly stocked. But for the moment Armando's avocado *ensalada* was the matter of business, and Gracie was loving it!

"Tell me about Willow Bend," Jean said. "Paul is so happy here."

But before Gracie could answer, she added, "We were as surprised when he felt the call to ministry. He'd always been the social activist. Miracles never cease. This place must be special. He's taken such a liking to the town, and especially the congregation."

"I'm actually from a town outside of Chicago. Came here right after I married my Elmo, God rest his soul."

Jean sighed. "I'm sorry. How long has he been gone?"

"Almost five years," Gracie said simply.

For a moment they stood in companionable silence. Gracie did not wish to dwell on the pain of her loss, so moved on.

Gracie picked up the conversational thread again. "Willow Bend is a small town. Wonderful people, but not too much call for ethnic cuisine. I run a part-time catering service and most of my requests are for fried chicken, potato salad and my famous candied baked baby limas."

"I am impressed with anyone who can cook." Jean reached for the paring knife. "As a matter of fact, I'm half afraid this salad will not turn out."

Gracie reached around her new friend to rinse another tomato. "I've had a whiff of that Honduran spice mixture, and if that is any indication of what this dish is going to taste like, you and I might be going into business together!"

"Gracie Jean's Cuisine."

"I like the sound of it. We've got The Sweet Shoppe and Abe's Deli and the Chinese, but nothing with a Latin flair."

"Until now!" Jean laughed. "Wouldn't Paul be shocked to discover his mother was staying in Willow Bend long-term! And to help run a catering service, no less. He was right to be surprised that I can cook."

Gracie looked at her incredulously. It was hard to imagine a woman near her in age not knowing how to cook.

"I was no June Cleaver in the kitchen." Jean apparently read her mind. "I loved playing with my son. My whole world revolved around him and Hal. Now Paul is about as talented at cooking as his mother. We both do grilled cheese and Campbell's soups."

"That boy does seem to need someone to look out for him," Gracie said. Paul had a reputation for being somewhat distracted, his head in the clouds. He was the bachelor all the women loved taking care of. She decided not to tell Jean that the ladies of his congregation brought him casseroles on a regular basis. They even did his spring cleaning.

What she did admit was, "Half the women in the church are trying to find Paul a suitable mate, scouting families for daughters, nieces or children of friends." Dare she confess that she had even thought of playing matchmaker?

"Hmm?"

Jean was staring at her. She felt herself blush that hideous shade of lobster that El had always teased her about. The kind that spread up her neck and across her cheeks. That blush her husband had delighted in evoking. She had let her mind wander again! "Heaven forbid!"

"Huh?" Jean was still staring.

Gracie stumbled through an explanation of her distraction. "Paul is so sweet. I know it's silly, but I find myself mentally matching him with every available female in town. I'm embarrassed to admit that's what I was doing just now."

"Don't apologize!" Jean laughed, setting her eyes twinkling. "Oh, Gracie, we are going to be great friends! I have tried to match that boy with just about every eligible girl I know. And I, too, have been scanning the church socials for ring-less young women. Now tell me, dear, do you have someone specific in mind?"

Gracie was really embarrassed now. "But we should let Paul find his own wife."

"That boy can't find his keys, much less a wife." Jean laughed again. "Of course, I also feel a bit guilty playing matchmaker. It *is* something mothers are notorious for, but you got to admit, Paul isn't taking any initiative. He'll be thirty next birthday."

Paul's shy grin popped into Gracie's mind. "He does have a certain boyish charm, though. He's the kind of guy we seniors love to mother. He's got a big following at the church."

"Smothering, he calls it when it's me." Jean smiled. "But he's told me he loves the attention you all give him." Another incredulous look. "He said some of the church ladies even took over his spring cleaning. Tsk, tsk. I quit doing his laundry when he was in high school."

Gracie laughed. "He seems to have it pretty well figured out."

It was Jean's turn to chuckle. "Come to think of it, he *has* learned to cook. We had several lovely casseroles. His freezer is well stocked." She looked at Gracie. "Don't tell me...."

Gracie nodded.

"I should have known!" A slow grin that matched her son's spread over Jean's face. "Now we know his *real* motives for entering the ministry!"

Jean went back to the *ensalada*. "I have to admit, I probably have spoiled him myself. He was an only child, so that's part of it. There are just more than a few stubborn apron threads still attached. I have to restrain myself from butting into his life."

Arlen had said the same of Gracie. It had been years since her son left home, but she still had to resist the urge to over-mother him, too, even though now that he had a family of his own. But she tucked the subject of El and Arlen back into that space she saved for when she was alone, and focused instead on Jean. "Paul had a fiancée. They broke the engagement shortly after he arrived."

"Lillian Peterson. Beautiful girl, but ambitious. She was studying to be a surgeon. Harold and I liked her, but sensed it wasn't going to work. Something happened between them—something he never confided. We were in Africa at the time, and, well, by the time we got back, that relationship was over."

"Africa? You were in Africa, too?"

Jean nodded. "The Sudan. We went to a missionary conference and heard a Sudanese pastor speak. God nudged, then prodded, and we went off on our first short-term mission. We've been hooked ever since."

Jean laughed. "It was uncanny. We got home from that conference and soon saw a notice about a mountain village in the north needing a mechanic, of all things. Harold is handy like that. Someone donated an electrical generator in need of some repair for the clinic. And in the same letter they wished for books to stock their newly built school library. I am a retired school librarian.

"So we spent three years, came back in time to catch the CNN report of the hurricane pummeling Honduras and Nicaragua. God didn't have to prod that time. A little nudge and we knew where he was sending us. We've never been sorry that we aren't taking cruises, or racking up miles on the golf course in Florida."

"That is amazing. How many assignments have you had?"

"Honduras is only our second. Hal had a scare, prostate cancer. So he retired early from teaching. He loved vocational education—taught auto mechanics. God healed him physically and spiritually. Gave us new vision, so off we went. The Lord certainly has been good to us." She looked at Gracie, her expression radiant. "So we'd like to give a little back. We're humbled that He's taken us up on the offer. God is good!"

"All the time!" Grace chimed her favorite response.

"All the time!" Jean had caught on.

Gracie grinned. "God is good!"

"Mom!" Paul's voice came from the living room. He appeared in the doorway, looking like an adolescent, sandy locks framing his face like a helmet. "Dad's puttering in the garden. Remind him that he's having lunch with me, and that I'll be back to get him about eleven-thirty. I've got an early appointment at the church."

Jean wiped her hands on her apron. She mock-scolded her son, "Going off half-dressed, just like when you were little. You were always in such a hurry—shirt not tucked, shoes untied."

She took a step back to give him a once-over. "It seems just yesterday your dad was running beside you holding on to the bike. And look at you. Pastor of your own church." She turned to Gracie. "We're proud of Paul."

Gracie was enjoying the display of emotion. "I think it's

nice, your having your parents here. A lot of young people wouldn't offer."

Paul smiled, plainly touched.

"We were having second thoughts about selling the house," Jean explained. "We left it vacant the time we went to Africa, but that turned out eventually not to be practical, especially when we were trying to make ourselves available for more cross-cultural service."

"Your living here just makes more sense. I bought this place." He eyed his mother. "Now, don't you say anything!" He turned to Gracie. "She's a bit of a nag about my finding a wife." His voice was affectionate. "She drives me crazy with that nesting syndrome of hers. Everybody's got to build one, right, Mom?" He gave her a hug. "I love her, though."

She pushed him away playfully. "I want grandbabies. You've got to have a wife to give me grandchildren."

"I love having you here, nagging and all." He pulled her back into his arms. "It's a perfect arrangement. You and Dad can go off and serve a while, and still have a home to come back to here. And this place is big enough to accommodate all of us."

"But if you get married—start a family...?" Jean said tentatively.

Gracie spoke up. "There's a garage out back with a second story almost begging for renovation. The perfect studio apartment, right, Paul?"

"Right." He looked at Gracie. "Wait! Don't tell me that you've been conspiring to get me married, too?" He wagged a finger. "Don't think I haven't picked up on the buzz around church! Marge is anything but discreet about her desire to see me married. Why, even the nice old ladies at the retirement home are scheming to marry me off!"

"Marriage is good, Paul. God invented it, lest you forgot."

"Mom!"

Jean smoothed her son's tie. "You have your keys, right?"

"The secretary gets there at eight, Mom. Pat will have the back door open."

His mother sighed. "Still misplacing your keys, aren't you, dear. You'd lose that handsome head of yours if it wasn't attached."

Gracie caught the flash of black hair and a white nightgown.

"Maria," Jean called, only to be answered by footfalls on the stairs. "Excuse me." Jean hurried past her son.

"What do think is wrong?" Gracie asked Paul.

He shrugged. "She didn't sleep well. Mom sat with her off and on all night. This morning I caught Dad coming out of the room. He told me she has nightmares. Perhaps the break-in's not the only reason. She's had a rough time. Another shrug. "Dad says they come less frequently now, but then there's a bad one." He paused. "We could hardly blame her, after what she's been through."

"That's true." Gracie closed her eyes and sent up a swift prayer on behalf of the newest citizen of Willow Bend.

Paul took her hands in his. Together they lifted both parents and child up to the Lord. By the time they finished, Jean had returned with Maria dressed in jeans and a crisp cherry-and-white dotted-Swiss blouse.

"Now let me get the brush."

A shy smile. "I can do it, Doña Jean."

"Okay then." Jean smiled. "You comb your hair and I'll fix your favorite egg tortilla."

Maria held the doll, face close to hers and, switching to soft, sweet Spanish, she seemed to say something similar to Doña Coca. As she attempted to flee, Paul scooped the pair into his arms and gave Maria a kiss on the cheek. "I've always wanted a baby sister."

"I am not a baby!"

"Of course, you're not!" He laughed and put her down. Maria darted toward the staircase.

Paul then gave his mother an equally loving kiss on the cheek and bid them farewell. Gracie leaned against the counter, basking in the familial closeness.

Paul left, and Jean turned to face her son's parishioner. "We are so incredibly blessed."

"That you are!" Gracie closed her eyes again for a moment, remembering those feelings she'd experienced when Arlen was home with little Elmo. "My El was fond of pointing out that we are blessed to bless others. I certainly can see that come full circle in your life, Jean. It is a wonderful thing you've done for that child."

"And her for us."

Grace understood the special gifts children offer grandparents, a more complex exchange when they also assume the parental role.

"You can't outgive God."

Gracie agreed.

"Hal and I have come to appreciate that all we have was already God's. You and I would probably agree it is easy to spend your parent's money—or blessings, as the case may be. God is a generous parent."

"I like how you think, Jean."

"We're going to be good friends!" Jean opened the refrigerator and retrieved three eggs. "Gracie, can you spare me a bit of that chopped tomato and pepper for Maria's tortilla?"

"Of course!" Gracie spooned some of each into a bowl as Jean put the small frying pan on the stove.

"Can I make the tortillas?" Maria asked, taking her place beside her mother.

"We're going to use the leftovers from yesterday. But, yes, you can heat them in the microwave."

When Maria laid the gray-haired grandmother doll on the counter, the brightly colored smock flipped over her face, exposing a knee-sized adhesive strip.

"Doña has a boo-boo?"

Maria arched her eyebrows. "*Qué?*"

In rapid Spanish Jean explained, and Maria grinned. "Yes, she has boo-boo."

"What happened?"

Maria shrugged, seeming hesitant. Jean rubbed the girl's back, while Gracie felt guilty for probing a tender spot, however unwittingly. Obviously it had something to do with the storm that had destroyed her small and secure world and brought her to Willow Bend.

"I put the bandage on," Jean told Gracie. There was a large and roughly repaired rip in Doña's chest seam. Someone else did the original repair, but Maria doesn't remember."

Gracie was curious, but didn't ask.

"Maria came down with bronchitis at the shelter. She wasn't the only one. The floor of the church was damp and cold, and most of those being cared for there had only the clothes on their backs. She was running a high fever, so the pastor moved her to the home of one of his flock. Sophia, the mother in that family, was a good friend of mine.

"Maria lost about a week slipping in and out of delirium. During that time, Sophia made a new dress for the doll. The belly wound still bothered Maria, so I played nurse." Jean looked at the girl and smiled. "*Voilà*, Doña Coca was better, and so was Maria."

An almost grin.

"She certainly is an unusual doll." Gracie stepped closer to Maria, bending enough to look into the doll's black embroidered eyes. "*Como esta*, Doña Coca."

Maria giggled at Gracie's attempt at reproducing the Spanish greeting.

"You speak Spanish?" Jean asked.

Gracie straightened to look at the woman and laughed. "About five words. I had a year or two in high school, but that was eons ago. I always wanted to learn some more. El and I used to talk about traveling. I've always wanted to see Mexico."

"I can teach you!" Maria's expression was eager.

This time Gracie laughed. "You don't think I'm too old? I am a very old lady, you know."

"A very *nice* lady," Maria corrected.

Gracie put her hand on Maria's cheek. "You are sweet. Your English is very good. Where did you learn?"

"I was learning in school. I used to watch television while my mama was working at the big house. There were English cartoons. I practiced much. Mama said understanding *inglés* would get a person far in the world. Mama wanted the best for me. That is why she worked so hard."

"What did your mamma do?"

"She cleaned houses for rich people. I stayed with her in the mornings before I went to school. The best school was near the big houses, and the big boss of Mama, his wife, Señora Martinez, she made it so I could attend the expensive school. Mama said they paid the bill."

"What a wonderful gesture!" Gracie wanted to ask more about the woman, but was afraid she'd be treading further on sensitive ground. Later, she would ask Jean. Instead she said, "How old are you, dear?"

"I have ten years. I have completed the fifth class in school. I want to study to be a teacher." She lowered her head, as grief filled her eyes. "My mama wanted this for me. She called me joy of her heart, her hope for the future. I was her only child."

Jean hugged Maria. "How about some breakfast now? You slept very late. In America we eat breakfast early, so we finished hours ago."

"*Café es bueno.*"

A warning look from the mother. "Coffee is not a good breakfast for you!"

"I'd like to try a scrambled egg burrito," Gracie told her. "Jean said you made the tortillas yesterday."

Maria grinned and went to the refrigerator. "I make them every day. I helped my Mama and my *abuelita.*" She looked at Jean. "How do you say in English?"

"Grandma."

"*Abuelita*, I like it," Gracie said.

With the tip of her knife Jean poked the pile of diced tomato. "Nice work, Gracie—just the right size. I can see you've had lots of experience."

"Lots of practice." She opened the door of the microwave for Maria. "There you are, dear. My, those look good! Much more tempting than the ones we buy in the grocery store."

Maria's expression registered surprise. "You buy them in the grocery store?"

Gracie laughed. "Latin American food is quite popular in the United States. That is why your mom is teaching me a few of her favorite recipes."

"Hondurans don't usually buy them," Jean explained. "They are such a staple the women begin early in the morning. They make dozens of them. They eat them with eggs for their breakfast—late morning, making it more the equivalent of brunch. They eat them with vegetables and rice for their big meal in the early afternoon, and as leftovers for the small evening meal."

Harold Meyer came in the back door with Herb Bower.

"Hello, ladies," Herb exclaimed. Noticing Maria, he took off his hat and executed a sweeping bow. "Good morning, Señorita."

Maria covered giggles, her mouth full of egg tortilla.

"How is the lovely Doña Coca this morning?" he asked. "I wanted her to know that there is nothing to be frightened about. We have a good idea who came into your house—boys, naughty boys playing a prank.

"My officer is going to talk to them today. Bring them down to the station for a good scare. Don't you worry, little señorita, Willow Bend is the safest place you could be. Don't you worry one little bit."

"Can I fix you a tortilla?" Jean asked. "A cup of coffee?"

Herb shook his head. "Sure smells good, but I ate a big breakfast. And the wife's been after me about my cholesterol. That cup of coffee sounds perfect."

"So you've determined that it was boys?"

Herb stirred a third spoonful of sugar in the cup of coffee. "Has to be. No other suspects. We talked to them this morning. They are an arrogant bunch, too—chips on their shoulders the size of two-by-fours. They wouldn't admit to anything, though. Jim is satisfied they were the perpetrators, and I trust his judgment. Since nothing was taken and there was no forced entry, there isn't much we can do but put a scare into those kids."

He looked at Gracie. "We'll do a thorough investigation—even in an open and shut case." Then turning to Maria. "We want this pretty little lady to rest secure."

Gracie poured Maria a glass of juice, thinking she'd try to find Chuckie and talk to him. She just didn't want to believe he had done it. And if he hadn't, someone else had. That reality made her very uncomfortable.

Herb motioned toward the counter cluttered with bowls and diced vegetables. "What are you ladies concocting?"

"I do not *concoct* anything," Gracie said with fake indignation. "Jean and I are creating avocado *ensalada*."

Herb shrugged, taking a big gulp of coffee. "Wouldn't know about that. Marybeth doesn't fix that gourmet stuff. Me, I like it simple—meat and potatoes."

"There's nothing simple about that," Gracie told him. "Your wife's a good cook, and I happen to know it takes her the whole day to make her wonderful Yankee pot roast."

Herb pretended to be cowed. "Now that you put it like that. . . ."

"So, are you going to arrest the teenagers?" Gracie said, changing the subject.

"Not exactly arrest. Bring them in for questioning. Scare 'em a little."

She was still not satisfied. Teenagers would not rifle through dress drawers. The prank theory just didn't hold up, but she didn't want to press Herb in front of Maria. The little girl seemed at home in Willow Bend, and Gracie determined that, if it was in her power, she'd do anything she could to keep it that way.

"Herb," she began. "I. . . ."

"Gracie, I know you got a heart for the misfits, but these boys are not Willow Bend's answer to the Little Rascals. Some of these teenagers are troublemakers. And, as much as you hate to acknowledge it, Willow Bend families aren't all perfect. Most of those kids are on a first-name basis with the truant officer."

Perhaps Herb was right, and she really didn't know the local kids as well as she might. But Chuckie hung out with them, and folks had judged him too harshly. She hated to have to remind the police chief of his prejudice toward those teens who were a little out of step with the status quo.

"You know, they could have been looking for money to buy a case of beer," Herb told her. "It isn't so out of the question to believe people may hide money in their bureau drawers—especially old folks." A hint of embarrassment. "No offense to the present company, but these kids probably consider you ancient."

Jean's smile was genuine. "No offense taken. But, Herb, I'm inclined to agree with Gracie. Kids would have gone for the computer or stereo equipment. I tend to think it was just curiosity seekers wanting to see if the pastor and his family were really human."

"We're still considering all the possibilities," Herb reassured her. "We just want to make sure you folks are safe."

Safe was a state of mind, Gracie decided. The only thing that was certain was that a person would always be safe with God. She quietly glanced heavenward.

G RACIE WAS THE FIRST to arrive for choir practice. She opened the door to the sanctuary, allowing its cool, gentle quiet to embrace her. She loved this place. It had old-fashioned charm, a contemporary ambience, and a distinguished pedigree. Founded after World War II and taking over the premises of an older church, Eternal Hope was a congregation Gracie considered the perfect place to sojourn until she was called home.

Deciding against turning on the lights, Gracie made her way to a cozy spot in a corner of the choir loft. The descending sun streamed through the green glass windows, spilling a soft light over the sanctuary. Gracie closed her eyes, grounding her being in the time-oiled oak of the pews. She could almost feel the brush of El's wool jacket, as he slipped his arm around her. "I miss you," she murmured.

Remember how we used to smile at one another. You out there third row center, me up here in the loft. You'd blow me a kiss right before the service. "Blessings," you'd whisper. You didn't believe in luck. Said everything was providence and if a person looked hard enough he could see the blessing in the worst of situations. I wanted to believe that when you died.

"I'm still trying, El." She snuggled tighter against the end of the pew. "And I hope you're watching me. I keep trying to learn from my mistakes!"

Gracie sighed in an attempt to loosen grief's knot, allowing the bitter sweetness to wash through her. It was grief that reminded her how precious life really was. Memories validated the value of a life, and El had lived it to the fullest. He'd loved and contributed to life. Someday they would be together in heaven and would look back over their lives, happy for the contribution they'd made.

"A life well lived, that's what matters." Her father used to say that. Even as an old man, crippled with arthritis, he'd praise God as soon as his feet hit the floor. "Another day, another blessing," he'd exclaim.

Remembering. It was good therapy.

She felt an invisible embrace.

"Thank You, Lord."

She closed her eyes again, listening to her soul, her connection to the eternal. Collecting together the snippets of pleasant memories, she could say with pride, *I've spent almost a lifetime in this house.* She remembered Arlen's baptism, and his confession of faith. It was a joyous mental scrapbook, each episode lovingly pasted in.

Penny-headed Arlen, fidgeting next to his dad. He was named for her brother, Buddy—officially William Arlen Stephens but always known by his childhood nickname.

Her mind went back, back, back, until she could see a strawberry-blond adolescent with unmanageable curls fidgeting in another choir loft, white satin robe tugging on her shoulders. Beside her was her brother, equally restless. Father and Mother sat as proud as you please, just as she had sat next to Elmo. The circle had come fully around. Arlen had played the same parts in the children's Christmas program. Tradition—a hang-on from the past? No, a springboard to the future. She liked that idea better.

It didn't seem possible that she'd outlived her little brother Buddy. He had always been so exuberant, taking life by the tail. Who would have thought cancer would cut it so short? She missed him, and made a mental note to call his daughter, Carter, whom she dearly loved.

Funny, it seemed only yesterday that Gracie and Buddy had been members of a junior choir. Her brother would jab her in the ribs and make her giggle with one of his witty observations about "the old salts," as he referred to the saintly members of the church. "The Saltbox" was his term for their church.

She smiled, recalling the last time she'd talked to Carter—

she'd used the term. Gracie chuckled, finally grasping the implication. Gracie had become an "old salt," all right, in every sense of the word. She patted her flaming hair. Yep, Carter could call her an "old salt." Spice and salt—seasoning for life. It was the best compliment a person could receive.

"Gracie, I'm so glad you're here!"

She looked up to see Marge scurrying across the sanctuary, with Tish Ball trailing behind. Several other choir members were beginning to congregate at the back of the sanctuary.

Gracie stood, realizing her quiet time had come to end. She closed her eyes one more time and thanked God for the nurture provided by memories, then walked to the front of the loft to meet her friends.

"Tish and I were walking in together," Marge told her, "discussing the luncheon, and Honduras came up. We've fine-tuned the blanket idea. It's the perfect project!"

"We are going to crochet baby afghans!" Tish beamed, her very blue eyes lighting up, and Gracie wondered if she'd bought the colored contacts she'd been raving about a few weeks back. Fads thrilled Tish—Tyne, too.

Folks never could quite believe that the Turner twins were approaching middle age. Blonde pixies, with a sprinkling of freckles across the bridges of their noses and a girlish naiveté punctuated by their giddiness, the Turner twins bebopped through life, merrily multiplying each other's enthusiasm. *Today will be no exception*, Gracie thought as she listened to

Tish prattle on about where they would get the yarn and how to reorganize the Women's Sewing Circle. Tish could carry the *esprit de corps* on her own, that was for sure.

As she listened to the pair, Gracie had to admit that she missed the sewing circle. She had loved attending the one in her own hometown with her mother, listening to all the "woman talk." She'd grown up thinking the Ladies' Aid Society synonymous for quilting bee. Her mother and grandmother had sewn plenty of quilts to help less fortunate folks during the Depression. "The Good Lord appreciates our willingness to get involved. No project goes unappreciated in God's eyes," Gracie's mother would tell her.

She smiled, remembering how often she'd quoted those words. Later she'd used the same words with an earlier Ladies Sewing Fellowship organized in Willow Bend. Gracie had fond memories of making blankets and layettes for the local hospital. They'd seldom heard from the recipients, but the knitters and crocheters had been faithful, and she was sure that God had appreciated their hard work.

Reactivating that sewing circle would be fun. Glancing around the sanctuary, Gracie suddenly realized she didn't even remember the difference between knit and crochet.

"I remember the blanket drive," Marge was saying. "They are wool. Warm and practical. I'm not so sure about knitted afghans. What do you think, Gracie?"

Tish was crestfallen. "Not afghans?"

"I think your idea is wonderful, Tish," Gracie said, hoping not to quell her enthusiasm with what she had to say. "It is especially good to get our church women involved. But it takes most of the winter to construct just one crocheted blanket. They *are* beautiful, that is for sure, but I am just not certain how practical that would be. We will probably want to send a lot of blankets."

Tyne Anderson came up behind her sister, dressed in the identical denim shirtwaist dress. She put her hands over Tish's eyes, and both broke into giggles, hugging each other.

As Tish brought her sister up to date on the details, Gracie began imagining a way to modify the plan to fit better the needs of the Hondurans. It was then Marge piped in with, "Baby layettes! Layettes for Honduras, that's it!" Marge clapped her hands. "From the mothers and grandmothers of Eternal Hope to the mothers and children of *Iglesia de Esperanza*." She winked at Gracie. "Not bad for cold-storage Spanish. I had four years in high school, then packed it away."

Marge was obviously excited, and Tyne's own enthusiasm was mounting. "Yes, that's it. We can purchase the sleepers and diapers and . . ."

"Knit booties!" Tish finished.

They grinned at each other.

Tish turned to Gracie. "*And* they don't take as much time as afghans."

"Some of us can knit, others crochet." Marge was thinking out loud. "Sounds perfect to me. What could be a better project than meeting the needs of babies? Church World Service has that blanket project, and I think I read that they sent them to Central America after the hurricane."

"We've got plenty of yarn," Tyne said. "We've crocheted sweaters and booties for the Women's Auxiliary at the hospital."

"Hello, all!" called Eternal Hope's tenor. Rick Harding put his briefcase on the front pew. "What is this I hear about sweaters and booties? I love to crochet."

"*You?*" in unison.

"Me!" A laugh erupted from deep in Rick's belly. "You think Rosie Greer is the only African-American male who can do needlework, huh? Well, let me tell you, girls," he said wiggling his fingers, "I've got nimble fingers!"

Marge put her hands on her hips. "We were thinking of a women's project, but I guess it *could* be mixed. That might be fun!" She smiled at Rick. "Who knows, maybe there are other secretly talented wool-and-yarn men in the congregation!"

"If I didn't know better, Marge Lawrence, I'd think you were obsessed with the opposite sex."

"Obsessed with romance is more like it," Marge said, chuckling. "What's wrong with that, *hmm*? Everybody needs a little spice in life. And romance—well, romance is *the* spice of life." Marge glanced at her friends, as if encouraging them to agree.

Estelle Livett turned toward them. "You know, Marge, men past a certain age are usually in the market for one of two things." She waited a moment until she had the attention of the group. "A purse or a nurse."

Gracie couldn't help chuckling.

Marge simply ignored the comment, perhaps not catching the joke. "Do you knit or crochet, Estelle?" she asked.

"As a matter of fact, I do," Estelle told her. "I couldn't help overhearing your conversation, and was going to offer my help. I already have a couple dozen or more pairs of booties finished. That's what I do in the evenings as I watch TV."

Rick rubbed his hands together. "This sounds like fun. When can we get started?"

"Let me run this by Jean," Gracie told them. Their enthusiasm was infectious, and she was developing a good case of it. She hoped it would be the same with Jean Meyer.

"Whatever it is," Barb Jennings called, "it will have to wait. Practice time! Hop to it, folks!"

Gracie took her place in the loft, as Barb played the melody for the new piece they were working on. It was a lovely arrangement, utilizing rich harmony, that Gracie hoped wouldn't be too hard for the group. Barb was a good director. The woman could get great music out of even the most timid of the singers, which often made their Sunday morning presentation pleasantly surprising.

Gracie complimented Barb on the piece, as the others were quietly taking their places. Barb was known for her no-nonsense sessions. She demanded their full attention.

Gracie closed her eyes to memorize the tune, enjoying the acoustics, thankful for this old church.

"I meant to ask," Marge whispered, leaning close, "any more word on the break-in?"

Gracie shook her head, eyes still closed.

"Nothing?" Marge nudged her. "Jim's so sure it was Chuckie Moon, Incorporated."

She felt herself tense. Why did her fellow townspeople have to be so quick to single out that boy in particular just because of his tonsorial peculiarity? After all, that whole group of teenagers sported mops in assorted Kool-Aid colors.

"They have had the boys in for questioning, you know," Marge whispered. "Nothing. Mind you, I think they cover for one another, and Jim says as much. He's convinced they are guilty."

"Innocent until proven guilty," Gracie reminded her.

Marge cautioned. "I know you don't want to believe anything bad about Chuckie Moon, but the kid is just plain *weird*. S-t-r-a-n-g-e."

Marge snuggled closer, her voice barely audible. "The dressers rifled through belonged to Jean and Maria, you know. Didn't bother anything in Paul's room. Now that's odd, you have to admit. What could they have?"

Gracie could only shake her head again. She was not going to get into an argument with Marge, so resisted pointing out that Harold's things had also been disturbed. The *weird* thing about this case was the fact that the two bedrooms were the only ones bothered. If it wasn't so illogical, she could suspect that they *were* the actual targets. But the couple had no clue as to why they would be singled out. Paul's parents seemed near saintly, so there was no reason to think they were not telling the truth.

Gracie opened the music folder at Barb's command.

"Gracie," Marge's voice was louder, imploring, "so what do you think? Got any ideas who else could have done it?"

"Girls!" Barb looked right at Gracie and Marge. "Do I have to separate the two of you?"

Estelle flashed a Cheshire Cat grin, making Gracie think of a smugly satisfied child. She closed her eyes, reminding herself to keep a good attitude toward the woman. She needed to remember that Estelle needed friends—and lots of encouragement.

Rick winked at her, as if to empathize. He was a darling man, and Gracie was thankful for his addition to the choir. It was hard to believe he hadn't lived in Willow Bend all his life. The easterner slipped right into Heartland culture. He was a welcome stalwart of the community, too. The computer technician had not only designed a web page for Eternal Hope, but also volunteered as an EMT with the volunteer fire company. And he *knits!* Versatile fellow, that Rick Harding. Gracie returned the wink.

That Sunday morning the choir sang in such perfect harmony that Gracie wondered if they weren't, in fact, celestial. The gravity of Rick's rich tenor set the tone, and Amy Cantrell's soprano gave it wings to soar.

"Beautiful, absolutely beautiful," Jean commented at the coffee hour after the service. "I don't have an extraordinary voice, but I can carry a tune. Do you think Barb could use another alto?"

"Of course!" Gracie gave her the particulars, but her radar was signaling: Stranger in the back corner. She turned to see a rather dignified man standing at the edge of the room near the exit. "Excuse me, Jean, we've got a visitor. I'll be right back."

Jean set her coffee cup on the table. "Let me go with you."

When Gracie sidestepped Marge as she headed toward the stranger, her friend grabbed her arm. "Did you get a chance to talk about the project?"

Gracie knew Marge would not wait for an update, so she resigned herself to the fact that the stranger would have to wait. Glancing his way, she spotted Pastor Paul. His radar must also have clicked on. He would take care of the fellow, she realized. It was natural for him to greet newcomers. She turned her attention to Marge, filling Jean in on what they had talked about before choir practice.

"I think it's a marvelous idea," Jean was saying. "I'll do what I can to help." She focused on Gracie. "Maria and I tried your cookie recipe. She had a good time. The child needs to laugh more. I'm hoping to get her together with some children her own age."

It occurred to Gracie, "My neighbors have that daughter about the same age. How about I talk to Suzy Hadlock's mother and get back to you? Perhaps you could come for a visit. I'll have Suzy over to play with Maria."

"Sounds perfect!"

Gracie looked for the stranger, but he was gone. Paul stepped into their circle. "Who was the visitor?"

"Evasive fellow. Didn't really answer me. Never did get his name, either."

Jean patted her son's back. "The preaching was good. And the music . . . I was just complimenting Gracie. Relax, Paul, the man will be back if God intends him to be here."

That proclamation had an uncanny ring to it. Yes, she reasoned, it was in God's hands. Yet, she couldn't help but wonder who the man was.

GRACIE PUT THE LETTUCE in the spinner. It would be fun to have company for supper, and Jean Meyer was becoming a good friend. Gracie had discovered that the woman loved gospel as much as she did and shared a fondness for many of the same musicians. With the exception of Marge, Gracie had never met a person so perfectly suited to be a close friend. They were kindred spirits, truly.

The telephone rang.

Arlen. Her heart skipped a beat at the sound of his voice. He and his family were the joy of her life. Did he know how much his telephone calls meant? She wouldn't tell him for fear he'd think her a dotty old woman without a life of her own. She swallowed her excitement and said in her calmest voice, "Hello, honey."

"Hi, Mom."

Something was wrong. "You okay?"

"Fine."

"And Wendy?"

Silence. Bingo! Something had happened between the pair. Gracie loved her daughter-in-law dearly, and didn't want to pry, so she waited for Arlen to speak.

"Mom." Another pause. Arlen had always needed time to collect his thoughts. He never was much of a conversationalist. Her only child had always been shy and sensitive.

She tucked the walk-around phone between her ear and chin, covered the salad and stuck it in the refrigerator. "It's nice to hear your voice." Sensing his nervousness, she went on, "I loved the picture of little Elmo you sent me. I put it on the refrigerator with the same magnet that I used to use to attach your artwork and awards."

She felt him smile.

"It's good to hear your voice, too. . . ."

Gracie sat at the kitchen table. It was time to take the bull by the horns. "Arlen, something's wrong. I hear it in your voice."

"Wendy wants to go back to work."

She heaved a sigh of relief. It was out in the open. But Gracie didn't know how to respond. Little Elmo was in nursery school. Sure, Gracie had chosen child-rearing as her career, but things were different now. Wendy was a good mother, the best. She would never do anything impulsive. If only she could see Arlen's face. "That's bad?" was all she could think of to say.

"Of course not."

Getting information from Arlen was like getting water from a rock—unless the person was Moses. She dispatched a prayer heavenbound, requesting permission to hit the rock. *Lord, let's You and I get to the bottom of this.*

"Dance lessons," Arlen went on, before she even had a chance to collect her thoughts. "She wants to resume her career."

Gracie was confused. "Take them or teach them?"

"Yeah." Arlen exhaled. "I mean, both. She wants to start a dance studio. Says if she doesn't return to dancing soon, she probably never will. Dancing takes stamina—and lots of practice. Ultimately, she wants to return to the theater."

Gracie remembered watching Wendy perform. She became fluid with the music, a joy to behold. Tall and willowy with penetrating eyes, she was also intense, a temperamental artist—the quintessential diva. But this daughter-in-law of hers also had a heart of gold. She loved her family. "Wendy's a level-headed girl," she told Arlen.

"Elmo's in school half days now. And there's space available on the first floor of our apartment building. I know she's really excited about this but. . . I'm not sure."

Gracie waited.

"It's a lot of money, Mom, to rent and set up a studio.

Utilities, advertising—it all costs money. Besides, Elmo needs her. I'm busy, so I can't be of much help."

She waited him out, knowing there was more to it.

"Mom, we're arguing a lot."

They need You, Lord.

"It's everything Wendy has ever wanted. At least that is what she says, and I believe her. But I'm scared. Beats me why. I mean, she says we can work out the money. We probably can.

"She'll be home when Elmo is, and when he isn't in school, he can go to the studio." Another sigh. "But I like her home. Oh, Mom, I don't know how I'm supposed to respond. I want her to be successful, really I do, but I like having a traditional family."

Gracie drew in a breath and let it out slowly. She never could come up with the right words when under pressure. She needed time to think, to pray. Arlen was a lot like her in that respect. He was obviously struggling with this. Wendy was so much like Big El—spontaneous. She interacted with life. She and Arlen were more likely to react. Thoughtfully, at least. He was calling her, and she had an obligation to help him.

"Mom? You there?"

"I'm here, honey."

"What should I do?"

"Love her." That response was easy. She thought of the bumpy times she and El had endured, remembering that love had required patience. And patience took practice; it grew through trial.

"I *do* love her, Mom." Arlen paused again. "Sometimes I look in her eyes and see all the promise and possibility we will share. I know we were made for each other. Then times like this, I wonder. She's so independent."

Assurance came softly. "Trust God. And trust Wendy. Pray together and the three of you will work this out. There's nothing you can't do with God, remember that, honey."

"How can I forget." A chuckle. "You've been telling me that all my life. Talking to you always helps."

"Talk to God, too."

She could feel him smile. "We will. We do."

She wished she could hug him, but settled for silently thanking God for her family. She had given Arlen back to God when he was a tiny babe. She'd been praying for Wendy even before she met her. Gracie had set to praying for the girl Arlen would marry almost from the day he was born.

Her children would be fine. Their future was in the Lord's hands. She braved, "Sounds like this studio is a good compromise. Wendy will be available to Elmo, yet have the career she longs for."

"Yeah, she really wants this."

"Then go with her, honey."

"Mom." His voice was barely audible. "I love you."

"I love you, too, sweetheart."

She held on to the phone a long time after he hung up. Her heart was full and tears welled up. If only they didn't live so far away from one another. She would give anything to hop into Fannie Mae and just drive over to their place. There, she could spend lots of time with her only grandchild. They would take long walks with Gooseberry. She would teach him to bake chocolate-chip cookies. She would get out her miniature teacups, and they'd throw a party for all his stuffed buddies.

She sighed and hung up the phone. If only New York weren't half a continent away!

Suddenly there was a rap on the kitchen door, and Rocky appeared. Gracie wiped the tears from her eyes.

"You okay?"

She forced a smile. "Great . . . !"

Rocky didn't look convinced, but as always honored her privacy. "Got coffee?"

Gracie started to fix a pot, and glancing at the clock asked, "You have plans for supper? The Meyers are coming."

"I'd like to," Rocky said, checking the cookie jar. "But I've got some editing to do. Hired a new part-timer—good kid, but a bit green. I need to check his work."

Gracie intercepted his grab for the jar. "So you'll eat junk food, right? Stay for dinner. I made beef stew—plenty of it. I've got biscuits and this tossed salad, so it isn't a problem to set for one more."

"What's that?" Uncle Miltie ambled in the back door trailed by Gooseberry. "You made biscuits. I love biscuits. How about fixing me one with syrup and lots of butter?"

Gracie clucked. "I will do no such thing. We're watching our cholesterol, remember? Besides, dinner is at six—you'll ruin your appetite." She turned to Rocky. "Both of you over-grown boys! What would you do without a woman to take care of you?"

"Throw a cholesterol-saturated pig feast, that's what!" Uncle Miltie snorted. "Women. Can't live with them and can't live without them."

Rocky laughed. "I've been doing all right for some time now, Milt."

"Yeah?" Gracie's uncle challenged him.

Gracie arched her eyebrows, giving her friend's rumpled appearance a head-to-toe sweep. She noticed a slight gap at the belt line. "You're about to lose a button on that shirt."

Rocky toyed with the dangling button. "Okay, I concede that my fashion sense is a bit lacking. But a man can mend— if he's got time that is. I'm just too busy."

"I've got time," Gracie told him. "And if you've got any other things that need mending, bring them too."

She set cups on the table and poured coffee. "Now, update me on the case. Does Herb have anything on the kids?"

Rocky shook his head. "Actually, they've got a pretty good alibi. It seems Chuckie is fixing up an old car and they were all over at Harry's garage. He vouches for them. He was letting them use his impact wrench to take off some rusted bolts."

"*All* of them were there?" Uncle Miltie asked. "There's at least a half dozen boys in that gang."

Rocky nodded. "Yeah, but the ringleaders are accounted for, so I don't think the remaining few have the motive or the inclination. They're not your most ambitious teenagers."

Gracie stood at the counter facing the two men sitting at the table. "So why is Herb still convinced these boys are involved?"

"He's had trouble with them before." Rocky took a sip of coffee. "Pranks mostly. Cordella Fountain swears they put her cat in the mailbox. She used to chase them out of Blackberry Alley. Said they were smoking and she was afraid they'd cause a fire—burn down somebody's garage."

He looked pleadingly to Gracie. "One cookie, please. I need a dunker."

"One cookie." She reached in the jar and retrieved two large oatmeal-and-raisins. "That is *all* until supper. And you are staying, Rocky—editing will keep."

A salute. "I bow to my commanding officer."

"Oh, brother!" Uncle Miltie scowled. "Another pantywaist."

Rocky gave him a jab to the ribs. "Look who's talking."

The men laughed, but Gracie was mulling over the break-in. "It doesn't make sense," she thought out loud. "Nothing was taken."

"Oh, yeah—there *was* something missing!" Rocky said, straightening in his seat. "I forgot to mention it. Jean Meyer discovered her cosmetic bag was gone."

"How about that!" Uncle Miltie laughed. "A burglar who cares how she looks!"

Rocky put his hand up. "No, no, there's more to it. Jean kept costume jewelry in the bag. Nothing of any value, though."

"I wonder," Gracie thought out loud, "whether this has something to do with Jean and Harold."

Rocky raised an eyebrow. "They did just arrive in town."

"And it was their bedroom that was gone through," Uncle Miltie added.

Rocky shook his head. "Wait a minute. It wasn't just their bedroom. They went through the little girl's things, too. Paul says he thinks his room was searched but nothing disturbed. He says he can't be sure, but he feels pretty certain."

"But why suspect the Meyers?" Miltie looked at Gracie.

She didn't know the answer to that. They were darling people. Missionaries. What would they have that anyone would want. Yet. . . .

"We really don't know them," Rocky was saying. "And they have been in Honduras where corruption, money laundering and other bendings and breakings of the law are business-as-usual."

"We do know them, Rocky," she corrected him. "They're Paul's parents."

Conceding this point, he said reasonably, "They may not know they're involved. Perhaps something was planted on them and the culprit is trying to reclaim whatever it is."

"Drugs?" Uncle Miltie was serious.

She didn't believe it. "You've been watching too many movies."

"Possibilities abound. Can't say that I'd mind a little bit of international intrigue. Makes for good headlines."

Gracie turned to the Crock-Pot. "All this speculating is not getting supper finished. The Meyers will be here soon and we can brainstorm some more. Right now you boys can give me a hand by setting the dining room table."

Later, after the meal the men washed dishes. That is, Hal and Rocky washed, while Uncle Miltie kept them company over another cup of coffee. Gracie and Jean retired to the patio in the backyard, where Maria was getting acquainted with Suzy Hadlock. Gooseberry rubbed up against Maria's legs. It wasn't long until all three were sitting under the weeping willow at the corner of Gracie's property.

Across the alley, she spied John Griswold dragging a garbage can. He stopped to talk to the girls and she waved, introducing him to Jean.

"This seems like a friendly neighborhood," Jean commented after John had left. "I wish that Paul's was as nice. There are quite a few rundown places around him. And he's close to the main drag. Anyone could wander by."

That remark surprised Gracie. "Willow Bend is perfectly safe. Why, we haven't had a crime since—"

"Three days ago," Jean reminded her.

Gracie wanted to remain empathetic, but she was feeling protective of her town. And she had an uncanny feeling the crime could have something to do with the newly arrived couple. "Rocky told me you had a cosmetic case taken."

"I didn't miss it until yesterday when I went to put on earrings. He probably also told you that it held nothing of real value. Strange thing is that it was a child's case— decorated with Tigger, from Winnie the Pooh. He's my favorite characater!"

They had the same sheepish grin, Paul and his mother.

Gracie laughed, telling Jean that she was partial to Rabbit.

"It does seem like a kid-related crime," Jean admitted. "And Paul did leave the back door open. Lots of them play in the park."

"That sounds logical."

Jean met her gaze. "We're not overly concerned, mind you, but I do wish Herb would catch the pranksters. Put a good scare—" She broke off. "Is that your neighbor again?"

Gracie looked where Jean was pointing, but the person had disappeared through the Hadlocks' back yard.

"No one uses the alley but the families whose backyards abut it. Could have been any one of them. Garbage day tomorrow."

Jean nodded.

A blast of barking and Gooseberry hurtled himself up the steps, diving through the cat door, with the girls in hot pursuit.

"A dog!"

Gracie reached for the broom, but the animal was gone. Suzy and Maria were already in the house comforting the cat.

Jean stood. "It was a lovely meal, Gracie."

Rocky was putting away the last of the dishes when they entered the house. Hal was getting the story of the attack of the black demon from Suzy. Neither had seen the animal, and had only heard a furious snarl, then barking. It had been enough to send Gooseberry over the edge.

"Bet it's Griswold's dog," Uncle Miltie said. "That animal is always loose! Did his business under the hydrangeas. A real nuisance."

Maria and Suzy said their good-byes, promising to call one another the next day. Gracie smiled. The girls were going to be good friends. She and Jean already were.

"Well, I've got to hit the office for a while." Rocky folded the dish towel.

Gracie wrapped the rest of the cookies in plastic. "Dunkers, for your next coffee break."

"You're too good to me, Gracie."

She and Uncle Miltie saw the company to their car. The

barking was fierce in the alley. *Pity the poor cat foolish enough to go out walking tonight!*

It had turned out to be a lovely evening, but Gracie's thoughts returned to Arlen and Wendy. She would send Wendy a card—and Arlen, too. Just a note of encouragement, telling them how much she appreciated them both. After all they were parents to the world's greatest boy!

7

GRACIE POPPED IN A CD and donned her headphones. Today she'd step up the pace with a jazz rendition of gospel "greats." She moved her torso to the soulful medley of piano and tenor sax. The artist sure could make that saxophone sing "Just A Closer Walk With Thee."

She was rhythmically striding down the street when she spied John Griswold retrieving the newspaper from his box. Gracie stopped short with Gooseberry on her heels. The cat hunkered down, as if expecting a canine aggressor to come barreling out from nowhere.

Gooseberry hated Samson, the Griswold terrier. Not that Gracie blamed him—the dog was a nervous wreck and therefore unpredictable. Most of the time he wore a big plastic funnellike collar to keep him from chewing himself.

Fortunately, this also restrained his homicidal passion for the local wildlife population.

Happily for Gooseberry, today the dog was contained behind the fence. The cat relaxed, looking at Gracie with his calculating yellow eyes, as if to say, "I've got all day."

"Seems like your little friend and the Hadlock girl were getting along quite well." He tucked the newspaper under his arm. "They visiting the preacher for a while, huh?"

"The Meyers are on furlough for six months," she told him. "They'll be living with Paul and enrolling Maria in school. Suzy is her first friend—and at this age friends are important."

"So they are."

Gracie bent to pet Gooseberry, whose attention had returned to the commotion coming from the side yard. Samson was now jumping and barking at a treed squirrel, his nappy head and pointed ears appearing just above the white picket.

"That animal is a nightmare on legs!" The dog ignored his command to be quiet. John shrugged, as if to abandon responsibility.

Gracie kept quiet, unwilling to say anything nice about the animal.

"Told the wife we didn't need another dog when Tallulah had to be put down. That beagle was calm. Terriers are high-strung, you know. But Betsy thought Samson was 'sooo cute!'" John made a frustrated gesture with his hands. "The name should have been the clue to the animal's delusions of strength. He thinks he can dominate creatures three times his size!

"But Betsy, she decided he was just excitable. She wanted a dog from the pound. 'A mature animal,' she said. Somebody else's *reject*, I told her."

John was on a roll, and he was funny. Gracie glanced at Gooseberry, wishing he could understand.

"Now it's *me* chasing the mongrel!" John punched the air. "Betsy can't control him. Stupid dog got away from her twice this week. And yesterday, he jumped out of the car window at Willow Mart. Went after some trooper or something. Samson can't stand uniforms—his previous owner was a security cop. The UPS man won't even come to our door anymore."

John crossed his arms. "Last night he dug under the fence and went chasing after something. Found him in the Hadlocks' shrubbery. Hadlock turned on the floodlights. Thought I was a burglar and came out with a baseball bat. Caught me on my knees trying to cover the mess that dog was making rooting in the bushes. What a night!"

Relieved that John had been the man glimpsed in the alley, Gracie offered her sympathy and then said good-bye before he went off on another tangent. Gooseberry had decided, she noticed, to head back home. He had gotten tired of waiting for her.

She put her headphones back on and picked up the pace.

It was a beautiful day. The perfect day for a walk in the park. She prayed through a medley of "What A Friend We Have In Jesus" and "In The Garden," lifting up the concerns of church family and friends. She prayed for Arlen and Wendy. Prayer-walking, she decided, was not only good for the heart, but also for the soul as well. Many people she knew would benefit by doing it, she felt sure.

Too bad Marge worked days. Gracie made a mental note to stop in her store. Marge had been urging her to see the new collection of "antique reproduction" jewelry she was stocking. Also, Marge was excited about a new line of greeting cards that her customers could personalize.

Gracie turned the corner as an ambulance zipped by, lights flashing and siren roaring. Up ahead was the police cruiser. Folks were beginning to congregate on the sidewalk in front of the church.

Gracie sent up a prayer for the unknown injured. She was practically running by the time she got to there. Lester Twomley stepped out to meet her. "It's Pastor Paul on the stretcher."

"Lord help us." Gracie watched them whisk the stretcher into the ambulance. Jean climbed in behind it. Harold had his arm around Maria. Her head was buried in his chest. She was obviously crying. Herb opened the car door for the pair. Harold guided Maria into the back seat and slid in beside her without saying a word. The poor man was in shock.

"What happened?" she asked no one in particular.

Jim Thompson came up beside her. "Don't know yet. Mr. Meyer found him on the floor of the sanctuary—terrible." Jim shook his head. "Imagine finding your son lying in a puddle of blood."

"Then it's really serious?" Gracie shuddered.

"At first, I mistook him for dead. Paler than a sheet. He's lost a lot of blood."

As they watched the ambulance pull away and the cruiser right behind, she felt herself go numb. Prayer came softly from inside her. She didn't have words but she was comforted. Paul would be all right, she just knew it.

"Terrible." Lester, one of Gracie's fellow choir stalwarts, shook his head. "Just terrible."

"Probably fell off the ladder." Jim's tone was matter-of-fact.

She turned to look at him.

"The thing was propped in the corner. Probably changing a bulb, missed his step, and fell backwards. Cracked his head on that old marble baptismal bowl."

"I was supposed to meet him this morning," Lester said, still watching the cruiser round the corner. "The Property Committee approved installing some new lighting in the pulpit." He focused his attention on Jim. "I'll bet that's why he had the ladder out."

Then he looked at Gracie. "Don't know why he'd be changing bulbs, though. We've got a sexton to do that."

Jim took out his notebook and scribbled a few notes.

"Was he alone?" Gracie wanted to know.

Lester shook his head. "I didn't see Pat this morning."

"The church secretary?" Jim wanted to know. "Doesn't she work Mondays? Where do you suppose she is now?"

They looked at each other, perplexed.

"Errands maybe," Lester reasoned. "Monday is usually Pastor Paul's day off, but it was the only day I could do it, so he agreed to meet me."

Jim scribbled some more. "So you met him here?"

"Met his dad, first. He was coming up the walk when I got out of my pickup. Seems the little girl had been with Paul, and now Harold was picking her up for a dentist appointment."

Gracie remembered, "Yes, that's right, Jean mentioned getting physicals and dental checkups before they return to Honduras."

"Anyway," Lester went on, "Harold headed into to the church to fetch Maria, and I went to retrieve my tape measure and clipboard from the pickup."

The little tenor glanced toward the sanctuary. "Thought it was strange, though—the front door being open. We keep it locked during the week. It used to be you could leave the sanctuary open, to provide a place for praying. The trouble is, you can't trust people anymore. Things change, I guess, even in Willow Bend."

He sighed heavily, apparently trying to accept that reality.

"Anyway, I went in the front door. Harold was already bent over the pastor. Scared the stuffing out of me."

Jim made a commiserating noise.

"I ran to the office to call nine-one-one. That's how I know Pat wasn't here. The office was locked."

"I'm going to the hospital," Gracie decided.

"I'll take you," Lester said. "That is if you don't mind riding in my truck."

"I think I'll go in Fannie Mae, then I can stay as long as I am needed." She smiled in appreciation. "But you can give me a lift home."

Jim flipped his notebook closed. "I'll just mosey around— ask a few questions. See what what I can find out."

"Is the pastor going to be okay?" Gracie turned to see Pat standing in the doorway, her face full of concern.

"Did you just get here?" Gracie asked.

"I went to the post office. It closed Saturday before I finished the church newsletter, so I brought the bulk mailing home with me. Took care of it first thing this morning."

"Pat Allen, church secretary," Jim said, as he wrote. "Arrived...." Wristwatch glance, "ten fifty-seven A.M."

"You're sounding like the detective on *Dragnet*, Jim."

Gracie stepped forward to put her arm around the slender young woman. "Can't you see Pat is upset? We all are."

Pat nodded, letting Gracie continue to comfort her.

"As far as we know," Jim went on, without looking up. "Paul and Maria were the only ones in the church. The little girl was in the bathroom when the accident happened. She thought she heard voices, but it could have been Lester and Harold."

Pat straightened. "Come to think of it, I heard voices too. Assumed it was you, Lester. Paul told me he was meeting you this morning. He was also going to return the Pavarotti CD he borrowed." She gave a slight smile. "I was trying to 'educate' the man. All he listens to is classic rock. He humored me by offering to listen to my CD."

Jim scratched his head with the end of his pen. "I thought you just arrived."

"No, I've been here a little while. Just finished cleaning up the mess in the sanctuary." Tears started streaming down Pat's face. "Just awful. I scrubbed, and scrubbed, praying as fiercely as I rubbed."

Gracie gave her another squeeze.

"So just how long have you been here?" Jim wanted to know.

Pat shrugged. "Half hour or so. Since I walked to the post office, I came in through the front entrance. I heard Paul in the sanctuary, so headed that way. But as I was opening the door, I spied Maria coming out of the bathroom. I stopped to talk to her. Then I took her to the kitchen for some cookies and juice. We heard the commotion and by that time the ambulance was here. I kept Maria with me when I realized what was going on. She didn't need to see that. Harold came and got her when they were ready to go to the hospital." She paused, struggling to regain composure. "I got a bucket and supplies."

Lester touched her shoulder. "You poor thing, so you've been in the sanctuary all this time."

"Maybe we ought to check with the hospital," Gracie suggested. "You've got a cell phone, right Jim? I forgot mine."

Herb was in the emergency room, and confirmed that Paul had not regained consciousness. They'd tended his wound and were about to do some tests—an MRI, he thought. Yes, the Meyers were still there. Gracie shot Lester a "let's go" look, and they headed for the pickup.

"Wait a minute." Lester reached into his pocket. "I've got to lock the front door."

Pat shook her head. "It surprises me Paul opened it in the first place. The ladder is in the supply closet in the back of the church. Maybe someone forgot to lock it after worship yesterday."

Lester was indignant now. "That someone would be me, ma'am. And I assure you that I did not forget. This place was locked up tighter than a clam—saw to it myself.

Double-checked everything, just like I've been doing for years."

"Then Paul must have unlocked it," Pat concluded. "But he never uses the front—sometimes he forgets his keys and has to buzz to get in. Funny, that side entrance was ajar, too. I noticed it when I went to clean up. I wonder why Paul had both doors open?"

Gracie was puzzled, and she didn't like it. She hated to think that what happened to their pastor was not an accident, but things were not adding up. They wouldn't know anything, however, until Paul regained consciousness, so for now her priority was to support the Meyers.

"Let's go, Lester!" Slightly startled, Lester quickly locked the door. They left Jim to gather information. Gracie made a mental note to check in with Herb. She had some questions of her own, questions she was afraid Jim wouldn't ask.

By the time Gracie got to Keefer Memorial Hospital, Paul had been admitted. She stood in the doorway of his room. Harold was in the leather recliner in the the corner and Maria was asleep, nestled next to him. Jean was sitting next to the bed.

Paul was connected to dangling bags and an intimidating blue box monitored his vital signs. Gracie said a prayer before entering. Her tears welled as Jean took the bouquet of daylilies Gracie had picked in her garden before leaving her house, and put them in a plastic pitcher she filled with water.

Jean could barely manage to deliver the medical update without crying. Gracie could see it pained Harold to watch her, so she gathered the woman in her arms, aware that he would have stood up to do so if he could.

There was still a lot of swelling, and there had been a dangerous loss of blood. Paul had been slipping in and out of consciousness, his talk garbled and incoherent. "Angry mumbling," Jean described it. He was sleeping peacefully now.

Gracie wished Jean could have made out something—a sentence, a word. That would give them some clue as to what had happened. It *had* to have been an accident. She didn't want to consider any other option.

"The doctor will be in shortly," Harold said softly. "Then we'll know more. Meanwhile, we pray."

Maria barely opened her eyes. "God already is."

"Hmm?" Harold kissed her forehead.

Maria smiled. "God is praying, I feel it."

Harold hugged her, and Gracie hugged Jean. God was in control, of that she was convinced.

Hours passed, and Gracie felt herself withering with the salmon-colored petals of the daylilies. She was not feeling as confident. They had not spoken for a long time; perhaps each of them was lost in his or her own anxiety. Gracie reached across Paul's chest to place her hand on Jean's, as it clasped her son's still fingers. She then reached for Harold's hand, closed her eyes and began to pray. Three kindred souls imploring God. Maria, too: four.

"Mr. and Mrs. Meyer?" The doctor had entered the room. "The tests were good—no brain damage that we can detect." He bent over the bed to check Paul. "He seems stable, considering the double whammy he took."

"A double whammy?" That surprised Gracie.

The doctor met her gaze. "Yes, Paul was hit in the temple first. Probably flew backwards, and then collided with what the police chief thought was the marble baptismal font."

"Let me get this straight. You said my son suffered two blows to his head?" Harold asked this a bit too loudly, prompting Maria suddenly to sit up straight.

Gracie was beginning to feel alarmed.

"Someone hit Paul?" Jean's tone was incredulous.

The doctor nodded. "That's what it looks like, Mrs. Meyer."

"Oh, no!" Jean started to cry again.

Harold was on his feet, this time taking her in his arms. Gracie moved to Maria, who looked frightened. She put her arm around the girl and reaffirmed, "Paul is going to be fine, right? That's the important thing. There isn't brain damage. He is going to regain consciousness any time now."

"*Ssh*, darling, *ssh*," Harold soothed his wife.

The doctor waited patiently, until Jean was ready to listen. "Your son has suffered a severe blow to the back of his head, involving a laceration. While the one to the temple was minor, there is swelling. He's in shock. The body is protecting itself, giving the brain time to recover. We'll keep him closely monitored. But yes, we think he will come to with little more than a terrible headache."

"In the meantime," he said, looking right at Gracie. "I suggest you take turns sitting with him, so that when he does wake up, it's a familiar face he sees. No sense in all of you staying. It could be several days, and you'll need rest too. You've all been under a lot of stress."

Gracie realized what was expected of her and insisted on taking Jean home. She would also take care of Maria until Jean felt ready to return to the hospital. Harold had already volunteered to do the first watch.

Maria didn't say much as they drove to Paul's house to pick up some clothes and playthings. Gracie tried coaxing her to teach her Spanish by asking the names for animals and objects along the way. Maria humored her, but her mind seemed miles distant.

"Paul will be okay," she assured the girl.

"I know."

Jean squeezed Maria. "Prayer is the best medicine."

A nod.

Her heart went out to this mother and her daughter who'd suffered so much. Gracie kept her eyes on the road, afraid she was going to cry, too.

"Heaven is better sometimes." Maria's words startled her, but there wasn't the slightest acrimony in the child's voice. "God takes the tired ones. He gave my mama rest."

She wanted to hug Maria, but her grip tightened on the wheel. Fannie Mae seemed to understand her plight and decelerated, stopping before the light turned red. Gracie reached over and patted the child sitting between her and Jean. "You're a brave girl," was all she could think to say.

"Doña Coca is the brave one." Tears welled in the corners of Maria's eyes, until Gracie finally realized the child did not have the doll.

Jean realized the little girl's loss at the same time, "Where is Doña Coca?"

A slight quiver in the lip. "I left her in the church. All of a sudden, we had to go to the hospital. Doña Coca is all alone."

"We'll get her," Jean assured the child. "I'll find the key as soon as we get home. Then you both can stay with Mrs. Parks, okay? That will make it easier for your dad and me."

Maria, finding this satisfactory, nodded.

One mystery solved. Paul's key was not on the hook. "I guess he must have it with him," Gracie thought out loud, as Jean searched the countertops.

"I could call Pat," Jean said.

"Or Lester," she offered, "he's closer."

They called Lester, who was able to give them an update on Jim's investigation. Chuckie Moon and friends had been questioned. They were claiming they'd seen a dark-skinned man with sunglasses sitting in a car in front of Paul's house. He seemed to have been watching the place. Jim, however, continued to judge their story untrustworthy.

Things were getting far too complicated. Baking cookies would be the perfect distraction for Gracie, but Marge arrived at her place within minutes of their arrival home.

She burst in the back door with arms open wide, offering the best and most comforting hug that Gracie could imagine. Nothing needed to be said. Marge held her tight, and Gracie relaxed in her friend's loving embrace. Tears trickled. Gracie cried for Paul, his worried parents, sweet Maria . . . Arlen and Wendy. It had been a difficult day!

MARGE WAS WIPING the kitchen counter when Gracie came downstairs after putting Maria to bed. "She sure is a sweetheart. It almost makes me wish I had grandkids." Marge grinned. "Almost, mind you, because *Gran* in any form screams—old, old, old!"

"Heaven forbid!" Gracie rather enjoyed the title of Grandma, but she was comfortable with her age. She had found each passage more exciting than the last. Yes, there had been hardships, and grieving for things that could never be again. But over all, maturing had brought more blessings than curses—with the exception of saggy skin and expansive hips, Gracie decided.

"What's so funny?"

"Gravity."

Marge chuckled. "Gravity. Does us all in!"

"It's harder on some of us than others," Gracie quipped, eyeing her svelte friend.

That pleased Marge. Gracie zipped the lock on the plastic bag of cookies Maria had packaged for Paul. The little girl was sure her new brother was going to wake up hungry. Gracie prayed she was right.

"He's going to be okay." Marge always could read her mind. "You've had a long day, too. Stress is more exhausting than physical labor. Believe me, I know. Fretting over some of my anxious moments, when things were out of my control, anyway, gave me more gray hairs than the drugstore has shades to cover."

She pointed a perfectly manicured finger at Gracie. "And you, girl, probably know *exactly* how many shades that is."

"Only the reds."

Marge leaned back against the counter. "You're one feisty lady, Gracie Lynn Parks, but don't you ever miss having a man to fuss over you?"

"I've got Uncle Miltie."

Her friend rolled her eyes. "I'm talking *man*. At this point in my life he doesn't even have to be tall, dark and handsome. I'll settle for slightly paunchy and balding, as long as the guy is sweet and churchgoing. You know. . . ." Marge smiled coyly. "You *could* have Rocky Gravino if you wanted him."

Gracie felt herself blush. "We're just friends."

"But you could be more."

She didn't want to be. El had been her all and all. Sixty-two and she'd outlived her parents, brother, more than a few good friends, *and* her husband. Yes, she felt alone sometimes, especially with her only child living so far away. But she wasn't lonely, for these last years her best company had been God.

"I've got the Lord," she told Marge.

"I know you do," Marge told her. "But don't you want to wake in somebody's arms? Don't you long for the thrill of passion again?"

Gracie let herself smile. Truth was she did miss male companionship. She did miss the physical affection. But she was happy with her life all the same. And she was *not* romantically interested in Rocky Gravino!

"I miss the intimacy, Gracie." Marge sighed. "I know I should be satisfied with life. I mean, I'm financially secure. I run a business I love. I've got Charlotte—and you, of course."

Gracie pondered words of encouragement. Recounting God's provision over a lifetime had increased her faith. All those answers to prayer had taught her to trust God's heart when she couldn't see His hand.

"Ben, my first, was a gem," Marge said, straightening. Her expression brightened. "He was a gentle, spiritual man. He said he'd be waiting for me at heaven's door."

Though Marge's eyes brimmed with tears, they sparkled. "I know God has been with me—on the mountaintops and in the valleys. He's held me tight through two funerals and a divorce. I should take your advice. Spend more time in prayer."

"You could take up prayer-walking!"

Marge flicked her fingers in the air, dismissing that idea. "Well, maybe. But you know I'm allergic to exercise. I have to force myself to keep in shape."

Gracie loved this friend, next-door neighbor and sister of her heart. They were so different. She couldn't imagine wearing flamingo earrings and Hawaiian prints. Marge would never be caught in sweats and sneakers.

Marge shared her faith, and that was the most important thing. They'd known the same grief, and claimed the same promises. They were kindred spirits.

"How about a diet cola?" Marge reached for the refrigerator door.

Gracie hated artificial sweeteners. "How about some homemade iced tea instead?"

"Sounds good!" Uncle Miltie appeared in the doorway. "I just beat Rocky at three games of chess."

Behind her uncle appeared the loser, looking all but forlorn.

"When did you arrive?" she asked Rocky.

Marge glanced at Gracie. "We've been out here in the

kitchen baking peanut butter bars for the last hour and half. We could have used a clean-up crew."

"We'll just try on a few of those." Rocky sat down across from Gracie. "See how they fit my waist."

They laughed.

"Stopped by to see you," Rocky said, looking at Gracie. "Milt was on the front porch and just happened to have the chess board set up."

"The rest is now history!" The octogenarian beamed.

Rocky scowled. "Bamboozled! I demand a re-match."

"Bamboozled, my sacroiliac! I beat you fair and square."

"You tricked me. What was that move—castling? I'm going to check the rule book."

Uncle Miltie wagged a finger playfully. "You just do that. Maybe you better study up while you're at it. Get the basics—like castling."

"I put in a full day. Up early, to bed late—story of my life," Rocky said, taking a bite of the cookie. "Up to par, Gracie, my girl!" Focusing on her uncle again, he said, "I just couldn't concentrate. And you, George Morgan, took advantage of me. Snuck that new move in on me."

Uncle Miltie let out a chortle. "Ha! Never knew a man who could scoop a good reporter. You're slipping, Rocky, and don't you go blaming lack of sleep. You're getting addled, pure and simple."

"Addled! I'll give you addled, you old coot!"

Uncle Miltie smiled smugly. "This 'old coot' can still beat you at chess!"

"Okay, boys!" Gracie signaled time-out. "Have another peanut bar."

Marge flashed her a knowing grin. "The way to a man's heart is through his underbelly."

"How would you know, Margie?" Rocky said jokingly. "Everybody knows your idea of home cooking is take-out and frozen fare."

Marge feigned indignation. "As Gracie's co-caterer, I'm not even going to honor that with a response." She flashed him a conspiratorial grin. "So, what's the scoop on this morning? Did someone hit the preacher or not?"

"Don't we get right to the point!" Rocky laughed.

Gracie poured herself a glass of iced tea and sat back down, this time beside Marge. She was glad Marge had broached the subject.

Rocky took a big swallow of tea, almost as if he were waiting for them to ask more.

"So?" Marge implored.

He seemed to be measuring his response, perhaps toying with Marge, knowing her passion for gab. "It wasn't an accident."

"We know *that* much, Rocco Gravino!" Marge stared him down. "Tell us something we *don't* know."

Rocky looked at Gracie. "It wasn't the the teenagers."

Gracie nodded. She'd known that all along.

"Then you're the only other person who agrees," he told her.

"So what do you think?" she asked him. She and Rocky were usually on the same wavelength. She loved that about him. He liked to play cat and mouse, a game he was almost better at than Gooseberry.

Rocky only smiled.

"Oh, come on," Marge demanded. "What *do* you know?"

Uncle Miltie put his glass down. "I got a hunch. Tell me if I'm on to something. That fellow at church on Sunday was with the government. I knew it right off, told him as much. He hedged, but I had him pegged. He's following the Meyers, isn't he? He's the guy the kids saw in front of the pastor's house."

"You've been watching too much TV," Rocky told him, but Gracie suspected he was considering Uncle Miltie's conjecture.

She met Rocky's gaze. "I suspect the Meyers *are* the target."

"I suspect you're right." Rocky's tone was level. "I think Miltie might be right."

"That handsome, available-looking stranger in the blue three-piece suit a government agent?" Marge tried to whistle. "Well I'll be!"

Rocky laced his fingers around the glass. "All the man would say was that he was passing through town on business, and wanted to attend a Sunday morning church service."

"So how do you know he's with the government?" Gracie asked.

Rocky chuckled. "Quite by accident. I was at the Willow Mart when this dog dive-bombed the guy. Jumped right out of a car window. About took his leg off—ripped a big hole in the guy's pants, then went for his coat.

"The owner, a frazzled middle-aged lady, was beside herself apologizing. She insisted on getting him a new suit. He wouldn't hear of it, so she pulled the jacket off his arm. His identification dropped on the ground." Rocky beamed. "Good newsman that I am, I was there to pick it up."

Marge leaned forward. "Wow! What did he say then?"

"Nothing. Just stuck the packet in his pocket. Grabbed his coat, jumped into a sporty black convertible and drove off."

"Sporty black convertibles stand out," Uncle Miltie said. "I noticed it in the church parking lot. Told Rocky as much. The guy is staying at Cordelia Fountain's. I saw the car again today."

Gracie's radar was piqued. "Today? When?"

"Coming home from the senior center," Uncle Miltie told her. "You were doing your power—er, prayer-walking."

She looked at Rocky. "Then he couldn't have been the man the boys saw in front of Paul's house."

"Hmm." Rocky leaned back in his car. "You think we've got two strangers in town?"

Marge put a finger to her lips, pondering. "Or Jim's right, and the boys made up the story. I don't trust those kids. They can be bad news. When they think of it, they harass poor Charlotte when we're out on walks."

"Well, this whole thing is starting to sound a little too far-fetched," Gracie pronounced.

Rocky looked up at her. "Hold on! It's not so crazy. Honduras has a corrupt government. They're notorious for international money laundering. What makes you think a pair of missionaries can't be used? They're the perfect fall-guys."

"So what are you saying?" Gracie asked. "They're involved with drugs, or money laundering?"

Rocky shrugged. "I don't know. Just thinking out loud. I do believe the teenagers, however. A guy who looks South or Central American has been seen around town. I stopped in to talk to Abe the other day. He mentioned a fellow with an accent coming into the deli. Didn't think much of it at the time. Then all this happened. Now, I'm real curious."

"Did you tell all this to Herb?"

Rocky shook his head. "Didn't start putting it all together until Milt and I got to talking." He looked at the old man. "That's the real reason I lost the game—you had me distracted."

"Poof!" Uncle Miltie brushed that excuse away with a hand stroke.

"And Gracie, you just hit a missing piece." He rubbed his chin. "I didn't factor in the car the kids saw. That's what made me remember the Latino stranger just now."

"She's a sleuth!" Uncle Miltie patted her hand.

"Sure is. That's why you're going to see Cordelia. Jim would go barreling in there, guns blazing. And that guy would recognize me. I know you can be discreet." A wink.

"Just what is it I'm to find out?"

Rocky furrowed his brow. "Don't rightly know offhand."

"Does anybody know where the other man is staying?" Marge wanted to know.

Rocky shook his head. "Didn't think of him till just now. We'll check with Abe." He turned his attention back to Gracie. "This could be wire quality. I'd love to get the scoop."

"Hey, we could get on CNN!" Uncle Miltie rubbed his palms together.

Gracie was worried the old man would talk. "You can't say anything, Uncle Miltie. This is hush-hush."

"Of course it is, dear girl! You think I'm a blabbermouth?"

She squeezed his hand. "No, I don't think that. But it's important we don't tip our hand. We all have to be careful what we say to folks."

"Hello! Reality check here." Marge scanned the group. "This is Willow Bend, small-town America—belt buckle of the Bible Belt! This is not Chicago. Not *Miami*. Come on, we're jumping to conclusions! This could all be coincidence."

Gracie had to admit she had a point. Why would anyone plant drugs on missionaries headed to Indiana? "You're absolutely sure the guy in church was with the government?"

"Yep." Rocky didn't budge. "Yep, he was government."

She was having second thoughts. "Maybe he was telling the truth. Did you see what department he was with? It could have been forestry or interstate highways—or some department that chases after delinquent taxpayers. . . ."

Rocky looked at her. "You've got a point. But what I didn't mention was the guy was sporting a shoulder holster."

"Now that casts a whole other light on the story!" Uncle Miltie said.

Gracie had to agree, but reasoned, "He still could be here for a totally different reason. We're not far off the highway. And Chicago isn't *that* far away. As far as the Latino goes, I haven't heard anything. Maybe he was just passing through, too."

"Could be," Rocky admitted. "But Gracie, my dear, I think you suspect differently. So do I."

She nodded. "It's worth checking out. And you're right, let's not tell Herb or Jim until we know more. It still could all be coincidence." That last statement rang eerily hollow.

"Well, let's check it out!" Uncle Miltie was the practical man. Action above words.

"We're not going to do anything tonight," Gracie told him. "I'll call on Cordelia in the morning."

Rocky nodded. "I'll pick you up. Let's stop at Abe's and see what he knows. Bet Miss Marple would like a bagel!"

Maria appeared in the doorway clutching her doll. "I couldn't sleep."

"How about some warm milk?" Gracie rose to fix it.

Rocky said something in Spanish, his arms outstretched. Maria scrambled into his lap.

"What did you say?" Marge wanted to know. "I know a little Spanish, but, *hombre*, you are fluent!"

Rocky spoke to Maria in Spanish again and the girl laughed, looking right at Marge. Marge put her hands on her hips, demanding an explanation.

"I told her," Rocky said, eyes sparkling with merriment, "that I would tell her a story in Spanish."

"And?" Marge cajoled.

Rocky winked at Maria. "I told her you would want to know exactly what I said, and that we were going to have some fun with you. And I was right."

Maria giggled.

So you speak Spanish, she thought to herself. *"Porqué?"*

Rocky repositioned himself to accommodate Maria. "I lived in Bolivia in the sixties." He looked at her. *"Me gusta mucho la gente."*

"He loves the people much," Marge translated for the others.

Rocky spoke to Maria in fluent Spanish. Her eyes practically danced in response. Gracie watched, her heart filled with love for this dear friend. Rocky said something and the child's expression saddened. She said something quietly, and then Rocky hugged her.

"She says her mama worked for a very important family. They were very happy, and the woman of the house gave her many gifts because she didn't have children of her own." He looked at Maria for confirmation. "She was the one who insisted that Maria learn English. Señora Martinez loved her like a daughter. And Maria misses her. The woman and her husband were killed in a car accident."

Gracie looked at the child. "How terrible."

A pair of eyes met hers, and a timid smile.

Rocky looked at Gracie, obviously concluding that this could be another piece in the puzzle. It was getting far too complicated for Gracie. Drugs, money laundering—it was simply too much like the plot line of a Hollywood thriller. This was Willow Bend. Gracie preferred to think there was a less melodramatic solution.

"Mr. Martinez worked for the government, didn't he?" Gracie asked, getting the background for Rocky.

Maria nodded. "He was working to make things better in Honduras. Señora always said that. She worked hard for the church to help the people and he did the same in the government."

The Honduras connection was a long shot. Maria's mother had been a housekeeper for a wealthy family. Tragedy had hit twice, and Maria was alone. Gracie would question Jean a bit more about Maria's family on the possibility there could be a link.

"You've been through a lot, Maria." Gracie smiled at her.

Maria managed one of her own. "I am tired."

"Sure you are," Gracie said, stroking her hair.

Rocky kissed Maria good night and added an endearment in Spanish. Gracie was touched by this unexpected glimpse of his paternal nature.

A feeling she was definitely not going to mention to Marge.

Marge hugged her. "Sleep tight, princess." Maria beamed, even as she rubbed her eyes in exhaustion.

"I promised her that one night I'd read her a story in Spanish," Rocky said. "She just happens to have a book." He grinned and stood up.

Marge told Gracie, "Well, I've got to get home. Charlotte will be worried."

"I'll help you load the dishwasher," Uncle Miltie offered.

There were only a few cups, so Gracie turned him down, reminding him he still had time to catch one of his favorite programs on television.

She herself needed a few peaceful, solitary moments to think, and the best place to solve a problem was alone with God in a warm, cozy kitchen. That had long been in the Parks family's "rules to live by"—and probably Gracie's favorite.

She also made a note to call Arlen.

ABE'S DELI HAD TO BE the best-smelling place in world. Gracie drew in a deep whiff of fresh potato kugel, one of her favorites. Rocky could have the breakfast special, but Gracie knew a treat when she smelled one.

"Hello, Abe," she called. "Are you by yourself today?"

The owner, Abe Wasserman, one of Gracie's dearest friends, was behind the counter making a fresh pot of coffee. He turned and greeted her. "Kugel?" he asked, with a wink.

"You read my mind!"

Rocky reached for a menu. "Why I look at this menu, I don't know, because I always order the same thing."

Abe Wasserman had taught Gracie much about the God of Israel. The Old Testament, which had been so easy for her to skip over, came alive with his telling. But he also was practical, logical and a sympathetic sounding board. Gracie often came to him to hash out dilemmas and difficulties, and she knew he always had the welfare of others at heart.

Rocky stuck the menu back between the napkin dispenser and the sugar bowl. "The special, please. We came to pick your brain."

"The special is still $2.95, but advice is free." Abe returned to the kitchen, where he could see and talk to them through the delivery window. "So, how can I help you?"

"Tell us about the Latino—the fellow who came in here the other day."

"You mean the one who ate my grandmother's chicken soup?" Abe came around the counter with the coffee pot.

"If that's what our guy ordered."

Abe excused himself for a few minutes to talk to a table of departing customers. Disappearing into the kitchen, he emerged again with their food.

"So, tell us about the Latino who was in the other day," Rocky prompted.

Their friend paused a moment. "Just like I said—ordered a cup of coffee and a bowl of chicken noodle soup." He turned to Gracie. "My grandmother's recipe, may she rest in peace. The broth is perfect! Just a pinch of mint makes all the difference."

"Umm, sounds good. Mint you say? Which kind of leaves? I've got mint in my herb garden, lemon, spearmint and peppermint." Rocky stared sternly at Gracie, attempting to discourage recipe chat. She just smiled, telling Abe, "I'd never have thought of it."

Rocky cleared his throat. "Did you see this guy again?"

As if to tease him, Gracie smiled sweetly and demanded of Abe, "What do you hear from Sophie?" To Rocky she said, "You remember—his sister lives in Cleveland. She's quite a cook, too. Bakes up a storm when she comes to visit."

"Sophie is Sophie. Every Saturday evening, she calls and asks the same things. How's business? Are you going to synagogue? Do they have a minyan?"

Gracie explained to Rocky, "A minyan is ten men required to do the service."

"Our congregation is small. People are busy. Sometimes even, it can be the same in church." Abe shrugged. "So, nothing is new with Sophie, and everything is new. She always is thinking of her family or new recipes to try—they're her presents to me."

Gracie loved his sister, too. Learning that Sophie telephoned her brother every Saturday was touching. Like so many other parents, Gracie had chosen Sundays to call Arlen and his family. She knew that, even when there was little to say, the sound of a voice over the wire—or whatever they were using these days—could be enough to lighten one's mood and one's heart.

"Back to the Latino guy." Rocky was certainly determined.

Abe scratched his chin. "He said he was just passing through." His eyes twinkled, changing the subject. "So what do you hear from Arlen?" He, too, knew how singleminded Rocky Gravino could be.

"His business is taking off," Gracie told him, "and now that

Little Elmo is getting older, Wendy wants to go back to work."

"She was a dancer, I remember. Pretty girl. He brought her in here when they got engaged, said I was the first friend in town to meet her. I liked her right off. But the grandson, how is he?"

She reached in her pocketbook for photographs.

"Please!" Rocky's expression would have caused lesser mortals to quake in their boots, but Gracie just rummaged for the envelope in which she kept her treasures.

"We've got a mystery to solve."

Abe shook his head. "Life's a mystery, Rocky. You know that. Don't be in too big a hurry to read the last page. The fun is in getting to know the characters."

"I've got a character in *front* of me, and another *beside* me. I've got all the characters I need!" Rocky shot back. "And I think we're getting well acquainted."

He gestured at the envelope of snapshots. "Okay, Gracie, I give in. Let's see the pix—but hold the photo album you've probably stuffed in there too. We don't have all day."

She laughed, elbowing him slightly. Talk about lovable curmudgeons! She showed Abe her newest pictures of Elmo and a portrait of Arlen with Wendy. Rocky crossed his arms, pretending to pout, but, at the same time, he craned his neck to get a good look at her photos.

Abe paused, apparently remembering something. "Hey, I do remember the guy asking me questions about our churches. I thought that was funny. He didn't look the religious type—told him so. He said he tries to worship when traveling for the sake of his mother. My sister, obviously, would approve. . . . Oh, yes, and I told him about your church, Gracie. I think he knew the name of your pastor. Yes, I remember that—he did. It surprised me, but he said he'd seen it on the sign when he drove by."

Gracie shot Rocky a conspiratorial glance. "Did he mention where he was staying? I don't think he's with Cordelia."

"Can't say that he did." Abe scratched his head. "Like I said, the fellow wasn't much of talker. Eyes were a bit sneaky. Thick eyebrows. You can learn a lot about a person by looking into his eyes. Windows to the soul, you know. If the man won't look at you, he's got something to hide."

Gracie couldn't help agreeing.

Cordelia Fountain was sweeping the front porch when they got to her well-maintained tourist home. She spied Rocky before he had a chance to duck out, and hurried down the steps to intercept him.

"Halt! Mr. Gravino!" she called. "You promised to do a feature story on my house. That was over a month ago. What's happening? I know it's something people will want to read about."

Rocky addressed her politely but sheepishly. "We've been busy, Mrs. Fountain. I'm sorry."

"I called three times! Your reporter keeps giving me

excuses, takes my name, as if he doesn't know it already. This tourist house *is* a historical landmark. Bed and breakfast establishments are cropping up all over, claiming to be the hotels of the past, but it's my Tourist Home that has the genuine stamp of authenticity, believe you me."

She wagged her finger in his face. "That newspaper of yours is sadly lacking in local color. This house was here before the the Civil War. Not many can claim that.

"It's about time you came to see me!"

Rocky apologized again, glancing around. He was hoping to spot the guest of Cordelia's whom he'd last seen at the Willow Mart. Gracie, meantime, complimented Cordelia on the planters brimming with geraniums. They looked stylish against the white building with its green shutters. Mrs. Fountain's Tourist Home was charming. "Picture-postcard perfect," Gracie told her, meaning it.

"I'm glad someone appreciates history." Cordelia glared at Rocky. "This house has been in the family for generations. Why, my granddaddy played a part in the Underground Railroad! But does your newspaper care? No! It doesn't matter that there's a tunnel in the basement. It's not story enough for Mr. Hot-Shot-Philadelphia-Newspaperman."

Rocky was getting an earful, with Gracie rather enjoying it. Then she took pity and decided to come to his rescue. "Some things just go unnoticed, Cordelia. I'm sure now that you've called it to his attention, Rocky will follow up." She phrased her question with special emphasis: "*Won't* you?"

"Sure." He offered Mrs. Fountain a placating smile. "I didn't mean to overlook you and your beautiful house."

Cordelia returned the courtesy with coy pleasure. "You know, Mr. Gravino, I am a member of the D.A.R. That's Daughters of the American Revolution. I've been the recording secretary of our local chapter for going on twenty years.

"And I'm active in the church. I served most my life on the Foreign Mission Board, so I certainly have interesting stories to share." She looked pleased. "But I don't want to tell you your business, Mr. Gravino. You need some more feature stories in that paper of yours, more profiles of prominent local folks."

"I do appreciate your helping me to do my job, Mrs. Fountain." Charming was a tough act to sustain for Rocky. The man rather resembled a tank, with a voice rusty as the tracks that move it. "I'll have a reporter call you this afternoon. He'll make an appointment."

Gracie smiled at Rocky. He could approximate diplomacy when he wanted to. She would compliment him later. For now she turned her attention back to Cordelia. "It seems as if you've got a full house. Is something going on in Willow Bend I don't know about?"

"Not really."

Gracie now chose to ask about the man she'd seen in church on Sunday. "Thin man, balding."

"Mr. Stone." Cordelia knew him right off. "Quiet fellow. Keeps to himself. He's always the gentleman, though," she said glancing at Rocky, as if in comparison. "I haven't seen him all morning."

"I don't suppose he said where he was going?"

"Why Mr. Gravino, that's none of my business. I would *never* question one of my guests. They leave the key on the hook if they want their room cleaned. Sir, he did not leave his key. He is obviously a private man, and I, for one, respect privacy."

"Of course you do," he said soothingly. "I heard he's with the government—and, well, I thought maybe there was story in it."

"The *story* is right in front of you." Cordelia tilted her head fetchingly. "That's what I've been trying to tell you all along."

Gracie was enjoying the interchange, but she sensed Rocky was losing patience. She'd experienced enough of his short-fused moments to recognize that he'd endured about all he was going to from their hostess.

"Do you ever have any international guests?" Gracie sounded innocently curious. "I also heard there's a Spanish-speaking fellow in town."

"Nobody like that here." Cordelia paused. "I did see a stranger in the park the other day, who could have been Hispanic. I noticed him because of the dark glasses. A man doesn't wear sunglasses like that unless he's hiding something. Mr. Stone wears dark glasses, too."

Rocky threw his hands up in defeat. "Another sage! But spare us the photo review this time. Okay, Gracie?"

Gracie laughed, and explained that they'd just been to Abe's Deli. Cordelia wanted to know about Sophie, and which flavor cheesecake Abe had on hand. Rocky leaned against the car in submission. Gracie and Cordelia chatted a few minutes more about folks in their church.

"So!" Cordelia was still determined to make the most of their visit for her own ends. "Mr. Gravino, you're going to send a reporter—*and* a photographer." With a sweeping gesture toward her establishment, Cordelia informed them, "She's a grand old lady! She deserves a full-page spread at the very least."

Gracie laughed. Cordelia was the true *grande dame*.

"I'll send a photographer," Rocky conceded. "I'm just not going to guarantee a full page, though, Mrs. Fountain."

She turned with a swish of her broom. "We'll have to see about that," she called, before going inside.

Gracie and Rocky walked over to the park and stopped to chat with a couple of mothers whose children were playing, but no one else had seen a Hispanic-seeming stranger. They decided to check Durant's garage, where Chuckie was still working on his car. But he was by himself, except for Harry, busily welding in the back of the shop.

The front of his car was jacked up where Chuckie knelt. Rocky stooped to see what the boy was doing. "Changing the brake pads, huh?"

"What's it to you?" Chuckie barely looked up.

Rocky gave a snort.

"Mmph!" Chuckie went back to bleeding the brakes.

Gracie stepped closer, giving the car a once-over. "You had it painted." The rust on the back fenders was gone. She bent to touch the front bumper. "Smooth as a baby's behind. Looks like you took my advice with the Coke and baby wipes."

"Yeah." He leaned back on his haunches. "But, Mrs. Parks, that's an awful expensive way to do things! I used boxes of wipes." The slightest hint of a smile. "Did you know it ended up smelling like baby powder?"

She smiled. Yes, she knew. Baby wipes and cola was her choice for everything chrome, including bath fixtures. "Well, your car's looking fine, Chuckie. What year is it, anyway?"

"Eighty-six." The boy wiped his hands on a rag, watching her peek in the driver's side window.

She nodded approval. "Upholstery is a little faded, but you've got air conditioning. Looks like a good buy!"

"Seven hundred bucks, not bad." A bit of interest flickered behind suspicious eyes: Chuckie was weakening.

She patted his shoulder. "You're quite the businessman!"

"Yeah, that's what Harry said. He's letting me use the shop and tools in exchange for my helping out when he gets busy."

She glanced at Rocky, giving her judge-not-lest-you-be-judged look. "Are you still working for Roy Bell?"

"Yep, when he needs me. Owning a car takes a lot of cash. I got to pay for everything myself." A nervous glance. "My family can't help much."

Rocky nodded, his expression turning sympathetic. "You're a pretty responsible kid."

"Guess so."

"Darn responsible!" Harry called from the back of the shop. He turned off the flame, and took off his safety glasses. "I told Thompson that. All the boys hang out here, so I've gotten to know them well. None of them went after the pastor—told Thompson that, too. That pastor of yours makes trouble enough for himself. He has a tendency to go butting in to what doesn't concern him."

Rocky extended his hand. "How ya doin', Harry?"

A grudging nod. "So what do you want with the boy?"

"The other kids told the police they saw a man out in front of the pastor's house. I'm just following up." Rocky turned to Chuckie. "Did you get a good look at him?"

"Nah, the car was parked in the shade. Had tinted windows."

"What kind of car was it?" Gracie asked.

"Crown Vic—burgundy. A rental, I think. Had the company's name on the plate holder."

Rocky took out a notepad. Gracie was a little startled by the spontaneous answer. Was Chuckie sure, or had he been rehearsing it?

"Name of the company?" Rocky asked.

"Didn't really notice, or remember. It wasn't important at the time."

"How about the other boys?" Rocky glanced up from writing. "Think they know?"

Chuckie bristled. "What's this all about?"

"You snooping for news?" Harry demanded.

Rocky took the remark in stride. Gracie sensed he understood all too well how the mood could turn ugly. *Diplomacy,* she wanted to whisper. But he was ahead of her. "News, we got plenty of that. Why, I was just talking to Mrs. Fountain about the recent increase in tourist traffic."

Though Harry Durant's gaze narrowed, he seemed to relax a bit. "Yeah, I've had more than my share. Lots of hurried folks with car troubles. The idiots don't watch the *idiot* lights—pull in with smoke pouring out from under their hoods."

Rocky laughed.

"Lots of rental cars through here. You'd be surprised." Harry glanced at Chuckie. "So the boys saw a rental in front of the pastor's house. You'd see a few of them, too, if you were looking."

Rocky didn't argue.

Then they discussed other local issues. "You know," he told Harry, "I could do another story. Louise McCall wants me to write an editorial on 'The Licentiousness of Spitting on Public Walkways'—her name for it, by the way."

This time Harry laughed. "She still on that kick, huh? That woman needs to look up more—she'd be less obsessed with what she finds under her feet. She spends too much time on those flower beds in the park, doing what we pay the city to do."

Gracie decided against giving her opinion on any of these topics. The flower borders had not bloomed brighter. She wanted to tell them that picking off dead flower heads was the secret, one she doubted the city would ever discover on its own. She was thankful for Louise and her one-woman crusade to help make Willow Bend more beautiful.

And, eyeing Harry, she decided he was probably one of the local citizens who thought spitting was a show of manliness.

"Is the pastor still unconscious?" Harry himself now changed the subject.

Rocky nodded. "Doctor says it takes time. The guy had a real trauma to the head. They think he'll be all right, though. When he wakes up, he can give us some answers."

"What kind of *answers*?" Chuckie got defensive. "Thompson thinks I did it!" He slapped the rag hard against the roof of the car and kicked the tire. "I knew the guy was baiting me! Did he sic you on me? The guy hates me!"

Rocky reached out to pat Chuckie's shoulder. "Calm down, nobody here is casting blame."

"It's not like you're going to believe anything *I* say."

"What makes you think we wouldn't?" Gracie wanted to know. She was a bit miffed with Jim Thompson for judging the boy. And Rocky's brusqueness was not helping matters.

Then Rocky surprised her with, "I believe you, son." He held the boy's gaze. "If you guys wanted to pay the preacher back for calling the cops, you would've sprayed paint on his garage door, or left a stink bomb on his porch. Your pals are way too cool to stoop to rifling through an old lady's underwear drawer."

Chuckie laughed. "Is that what really happened? Thompson made it sound like the place was ransacked."

"Thompson's been watching too many cop show reruns."

Gracie gave her friend "the eyebrows," as El used to call her look of special disapproval. "*Officer* Thompson is only doing his job. The bureau drawers *were* a mess." She smiled at Chuckie. "I do believe you, too. We've been through a lot, you and I."

"Yeah, I've done some stupid things." His shoulders drooped a little. "I behave like a jerk sometimes, but I'd never do anything illegal. Well, *seriously* illegal." He looked at her with all sincerity. "Mrs. Parks, I *am* really working on that temper of mine."

She put her hand on his shoulder. "I believe you. We need your help." He brightened, and she went on, "If you remember the name of the rental agency, or see that car again, will you call one of us?"

"Sure, Mrs. Parks, I can do that."

Rocky took out a business card and handed it to the boy. "Here you go, Chuck, talk to your friends, see what you can find out and give me a call. If you like, I'll treat you to pizza or something."

They walked back to his car and Rocky asked, "You really believe him, Gracie?"

"Yes." Her answer was easy.

Rocky grunted, then changed the subject. "I admire the way you handle people. You were wonderful with Mrs. Fountain, by the way. And now we have a friend in Chuckie Moon. I have a feeling he'll find something and call us. You're amazing, Gracie Parks."

"A gentle word turns away wrath."

"More Old Testament wisdom?"

"Right on." She smiled. "Proverbs."

He raised an eyebrow. "I'll have to read it."

For a man who didn't espouse faith, Rocky certainly was full of surprises.

10

WHEN CHURCH FOLKS get together to solve something, the solution is often more complicated than the problem. Gracie rubbed her temples. She'd endured enough bickering to last a week!

Estelle sat prim and proper, lips pursed in self-righteous indignation. Tish and Tyne were on the verge of tears. All poor Rick Harding wanted was to knit-one-purl-two. The newly reformed sewing circle was at an impasse, and they hadn't created even one layette for Honduras!

"Does it really matter if the booties are knitted or crocheted?" Marybeth Bowers' question was timid.

Tyne squeezed her sister's hand. "Can't we do both?"

"Both would be nice," Tish agreed.

Estelle crossed her arms. "They should all be the same. Continuity! That is the important thing."

"Continuity," the twins agreed in unison.

"Conformity is more like it." Marge leaned forward. "Conformity is next to godliness in your book, isn't it, Estelle?" She let out an impatient sniff. "The important thing is that those babies get layettes."

Marybeth Bower sat wringing her hands.

Rick Harding moved from his spot by the refreshment table. "Now, now, ladies. We've been all through this. We're not going to solve this by attacking each other."

"No one's attacking anyone." Marge practically spat the words.

Estelle straightened. "Knitted booties are warmer—easier to do. And *most* of us can knit!"

"I can't knit!" Marge was in her face.

Estelle glared back. "You can learn!"

"It's easy," Marybeth said timidly. "I'm not very good but I could teach you."

Rick jumped in. "I'll teach you, Marge. It's a piece of cake."

"A man teach me?" Marge's voice turned patronizing. "I've crocheted bedspreads—prize-winning afghans."

Gracie had had enough. "This isn't a competition. We're trying to help people who have lost everything. Does it really matter if we crochet or knit? I'm not good at either, but I'm willing to do whichever. The *important* thing is that we do something."

"You're right," Estelle conceded, but flashed a condescending look to Marge. "We could do both." A sigh. "Even if both aren't as practical."

Marge flopped back in the chair. "I don't have to participate."

"Of course you do." Gracie was tired of conflict, and implored her friend with her eyes. "It was your idea—and a great idea. Marge, we're best neighbors and buddies, and we do practically everything together. It wouldn't be the same working on this without *you*."

"We'll take a vote," Tish announced.

Tyne jumped up. "How many for crocheted booties?"

Estelle cleared her throat. "If we're going to take a vote let us do it decently and in order. The motion is that all the booties should be the same."

Marge let out a sigh of exasperation. "That puts us back at at square one, Estelle, because not all of us can knit, remember?"

"Okay," Gracie took the bull by the horns. "The vote is for continuity! We either crochet or knit, not both."

Rick joined her, "Hands for continuity."

Tish and Tyne looked at each other, then raised hands in unison.

Estelle's hand shot up. "That's three! Marybeth, what about you? How do you vote?"

"I don't know." Marybeth chewed her bottom lip. "Can I abstain?"

Marge threw her hands up.

"That still leaves three to three," Rick pointed out. Then looked at Gracie. "Unless you're also abstaining."

"Well, dear chum," Marge said to her, "which will it be? I'm not going to learn to knit."

Gracie wanted peace, but there could be no compromise for either Estelle or Marge. If she voted her heart, Estelle would be mad. If she voted for practicality, Marge would be mad. She sent up a silent plea for wisdom.

"Let's do both." Estelle was willing to see the light—just as long as she was the one holding the torch. "It seems to be the only solution."

Tyne and Tish now nodded their heads.

Marge's "Thanks," was tenuous, but at least she'd said it.

Gracie breathed easy again.

"But," Estelle began, straightening her shoulders, "there will be continuity. Boys' layettes knitted and the girls' crocheted."

"We can live with that." Gracie looked at Marge imploringly.

Marge rolled her eyes but agreed to it.

"Let's have those refreshments," Rick exclaimed. He began pouring glasses of lemonade. "To compromise!"

They all joined him in the toast.

Gracie looked heavenward. *Thank You, Lord.*

Tish began making an insert for the bulletin explaining the project, and requesting donations of sleepers, diapers, undershirts and receiving blankets. Marge had made peace with Estelle, and now they were discussing how to package the kits with Marybeth. Gracie decided to start to clean up, happy that it had turned out to be a productive morning after all.

Rick joined her. "I thought I'd put something on the church Web site. Do an interview with the Meyers, and Maria in particular. Maybe other churches will want to get involved. What do you think?"

"I think it's a great idea." Gracie paused, glancing at the newly formed "Layettes for Honduras" group, and praying that this would be the first project of many, despite their wobbly beginning.

Pastor Paul would be proud. He had been crusading his congregation for more active participation in mission since he'd come almost three years earlier. She could now understand that a lot of that zeal was hereditary. Gracie looked forward to updating her new friend on their progress. It would help take Jean's mind off her son.

Gracie intercepted him before Rick could begin picking up precariously stacked cups. "I'll get those. You put the cookies back in the containers."

"You'd think I was a klutz!" He was grinning.

She didn't have the heart to tell him that his reputation had preceded him. In spite of his capability cruising cyberspace and his knack at knitting, the man was clumsy. The Eternal Hope kitchen crew had learned that, two vases and several glasses late. Now, they steered the goodhearted fellow to less dangerous tasks.

"The containers are marked," Gracie told him, "for easy storage in my freezer."

"I like to freeze, too. We have a garden," he said, packaging the cookies. "Freezing the abundance is recreational therapy."

Gracie was fond of his wife, who was a nurse-anesthetist, and their two-year-old daughter. "So how do you manage it—working, parenting, volunteering at the church and still having time to can and preserve?"

"I'm Mr. Mom." He grinned. "No, seriously, I can work out of the house. That's the beauty of computers. I just check in at the office now and then and attend meetings."

Gracie was intrigued. "So tell me how the two of you worked it out. Or has your job always been like that."

"No, that's part of the reason I took this one—it afforded me flexible hours. I'm a night person and do most of my work on the computer. As you're discovering, I also love homemaking. Grandma taught me everything she knew."

Rick chuckled, pausing a moment to reflect. "I miss my loving, cantankerous grandma. She was one special woman—

practically raised us because Ma worked long hours. Grandma said she was raising us to be tough on the outside, tender on the inside.

"'Ain't no reason a black man can't learn to fry chicken,' she'd say."

"Did you learn?" Gracie wanted to know, enjoying his reminiscence.

A bright grin. "Why, you're just going have to come over for dinner some night and find out." Rick stacked the containers in Gracie's oversized basket.

"Like I was saying," he continued. "Homemaking comes easily to me. And Comfort hates it. Don't get me wrong; she's a wonderful mother—dotes on Lillian. I usually cook supper. She helps with dishes and does Lillian's evening bath. We both put our little angel to bed. Neither of us would miss that."

Theirs seemed a perfect parenting arrangement. Their model might also work for Arlen and Wendy. Arlen always loved to help in the kitchen, and she'd seen him do laundry. But Arlen's job was not quite so flexible. "My son and his wife are trying to navigate dual careers and a family." She looked at Rick. "They're having some trouble."

"It isn't easy." He caught her gaze. "I don't mean to sound like we don't struggle. We both had to sacrifice pride, and, I'm not ashamed to say, I'm taking it to the altar just about every day."

Gracie understood. Only too well. Arlen had inherited his

stubborn nature from her. She'd fallen off her high horse plenty of times. It was El who picked her up, forgiving her and encouraging her to go on that had made the difference in their marriage. "It took me a long time to learn pride is sin."

"I'm still learning it." He laughed. "I think Comfort would tell you the same. She considers herself Super Mom, so it's been extra hard for her to give up control.

"Especially when she runs into some of the stay-at-home moms. They say things without thinking, giving her the impression they look down on her because they think she chose her career over mothering."

Gracie felt protective of Wendy—and Comfort. "But she didn't have to choose one or the other. You've worked it out between yourselves."

"That's what I tell her." He leaned against the counter. "The thing is, Gracie, it's still tough. My boss expects me to be more available. I want her to pick up the slack. Lillian gets sick, and only Mommy can comfort her."

Gracie put dishes in the sink. "So what do you advise? What should tell I Arlen and Wendy?"

"Parenting isn't fifty/fifty. It's not even seventy/thirty." He reached for a towel. "You have to be willing to give one hundred percent, one hundred *fifty*. We have a tendency to want to divvy things up. We want to be *fair*. But mothering and fathering isn't always fair."

Gracie could see his point. "Marriage isn't always fair

either. It only needs to be just. We are equal partners, but sometimes one person has to give more than the other. That isn't equal, but it is the way it has be. The next time the other partner may have to give."

"Yeah, that's it. In the long run, love balances the scales." Gracie smiled her agreement.

Rick took a cup out of the drainer and began to dry. "Don't worry, I'll be careful."

"You're a delight, Rick Harding. I'm glad you relocated in Willow Bend."

"Me, too." Putting the cup away he went on, "Comfort and I decided to stop keeping track, figuring what was fair and what wasn't. Sometimes I've got to be out of town a few days, so she takes time off. I covered for her when she went to that convention in Florida."

"I wish you could talk to Arlen." She paused, thinking how different a community her son and his wife had in the East. She knew they went to church, but it was one of those big, program-oriented places. Everybody associated with peers, the career parents, middlers, senior citizens; each group had its specialized programs. The ministry seemed to target age more than need, Gracie had thought. But she'd kept her feelings to herself, appreciating Eternal Hope all the more.

"We need more family churches," she declared. "Places where generations mix, where older couples befriend newly-weds, seniors adopt grandkids, and men join sewing circles."

Rick chuckled. "That's another reason we moved from the East Coast. We wanted that kind of community."

He paused, looking at her. "They say it takes a village to raise a child, but I think the problem is that we've lost the village. Big cities or open space, neither facilitates family."

She looked into his honest face, admiring his decency. The man was wise beyond his thirty-something years.

"Comfort and I found suburbia grimly solitary. Church was a half-hour drive away, and everyone was too busy for community."

"Small towns can be parochial, too," she warned him. "We don't always see the need, and we sometimes shut out the lonely ones unintentionally."

She was thinking of the once green-haired Chuckie, and thankful for men like Harry who were willing to be color-blind. Gracie hated to admit that on occasion she'd judged the man as narrow-minded. He was a sound fellow, though, underneath it all, and a mentor to the teenaged boys.

Marybeth appeared in the doorway. "You'll be happy to know, we have it all worked out. We've formed buddy groups. Estelle is going to help you, Gracie." She smiled. "You did say you were a little rusty."

Gracie agreed.

"Tish and Tyne and I are going to be a threesome," Marybeth added. "They're talented, but I'm a just a beginner."

"And *Rick*," she lowered her voice, "We put you with Marge. She thinks she can teach you a few things."

Rick's affirmation was gracious. Gracie imagined him to be a man of many talents, of which knitting and crocheting were only minor attainments.

"Oh, I almost forgot. We're going to open the circle with devotions. We were hoping one of you would do it when we next get together."

Gracie looked at Rick.

"Knit one—purl Psalms!" Rick grinned. "I'll be happy to take the first one."

Gracie stopped to check in on Paul at the hospital after the meeting. Jean was sitting beside his bed, so she pulled up a chair. Gracie could almost not bear looking at the pale figure attached to the complex apparatus, so she surveyed the room. A half dozen bouquets of flowers lined the window overlooking the parking lot, and someone (probably his mother) had pinned all the cards to a bedside bulletin board. "Lots of well wishers."

"Lots of prayers," Jean answered.

Gracie faced her sadness and looked at Paul. "How is he?" A stray lock of sandy hair overlapped his eyebrow. She reached to brush it out of his face. "Any change?"

"He's semi-conscious. He mumbles, tries to focus and then drifts back to wherever he is." Jean's lips wore the "mother smile," an expression that reminded Gracie of past bedside vigils with Arlen during his childhood illnesses. She could well appreciate the gentle hand of this woman, whose maternal devotion was steady and true. As the slumbering Paul must have felt soothed, so did Gracie, watching them.

"Children belong to everyone," she thought out loud. Jean nodded. Mercy flowed unspoken between them.

Mother love. It warmed her soul to share it with Jean.

"The doctor says this stop-and-go progress is common with head injuries," her friend said after a while. "I just wish he'd wake up for even a moment. I'd give anything for his smile."

She brushed tears from her cheek. There seemed no further need for words. They sat in easy silence until Gracie spoke with all the concern of her heart, "How are you holding up?"

"Best as can be expected." A slight smile. "Thanks for the peanut-butter bars, by the way. I'm sorry I wasn't there to see you when you brought Maria back."

"She's a godsend for us during all this. Harold had her here earlier. She pinned up the cards."

Gracie should have known. "Maria was tickled to make those cookie bars. She wanted the recipe. It was her suggestion to bag them for Paul and her dad."

"When you brought her home she had Harold and Doña Coca sit down to cookies and milk." Jean was laughing now. "Doña Coca even reminded him to watch his sugar intake."

Her expression turned a bit more serious. "Harold's diabetic, you know."

She didn't know. Cancer *and* diabetes. And the man had been serving in Third World countries. Paul's parents were truly exceptional. "I've felt so helpless," she told Jean. "Seeing Paul like this makes me want to cry."

"I've cried enough for both of us." Jean squeezed her hand.

The unexpectedness of their circumstances hit her once again. "Who would do a thing like this?"

Jean shook her head. Her quiet groan was deep.

Gracie was hesitant to ask what she so longed to know. "Could any of this possibly have been directed at you or Harold?"

"Us?" Jean stared blankly.

Gracie took a breath. "Could anyone have put something in your luggage—something in your carry-on?"

"You sound like airport security!"

Jean looked away, not saying anything for several long minutes.

"I didn't mean to imply—"

Jean met her gaze. "The thought *has* crossed our minds. I brought it up with Officer Thompson, and we even searched the lining of our suitcases. Checked everything, but there was nothing suspicious."

Gracie searched her mind. "What about the missing cosmetic bag? Could there have been anything in it?"

"No, I know there wasn't. I don't own anything of value but the rings on my fingers." Jean paused, apparently rethinking her response. "No, there was nothing extra in it, I'm sure of it."

Gracie was grasping at straws. "And no one had access to your luggage?"

"Pastor Reyes took us to the airport—a dear Christian man. He helped us with our bags, and no one else handled them." Jean looked at Gracie. "I have to admit, this whole thing has scared me. I have been racking my brain for some explanation. Why would anyone attack Paul?"

If only he would wake up! If only Paul could tell them what really happened! For the time being, no one could feel safe until the case was solved. For everyone's sake, she needed to probe a bit more. "Would anyone be looking for Maria? A Latino has been asking around. He mentioned Paul by name."

"Paul has lots of international friends. He has always been quite involved in missionary work."

Gracie next asked, "What about Maria?"

"Her closest family was killed in the landslide. As far as I know, there's only an uncle. A drifter. He'd never have money to come to the United States, much less any inclination to look up Maria."

Jean shook her head. "No, there's no one else in Maria's life. We checked before the adoption."

"How about the family her mother worked for? Maria says they were both killed in an accident. Is there a chance it wasn't an accident?"

Jean pondered that a moment. "Carlos Martinez *was* a powerful man from one of Tegucigalpa's wealthiest families. He was charged with taking bribes, so there is mystery surrounding the accident. But Gracie, how would Maria play into it? Her mom was just a housekeeper."

"Perplexing."

Jean nodded, focusing her attention on her son. "Jim Thompson still suspects the skateboard gang, but he says they all have alibis. He's going to talk to the boy with the green hair."

Gracie made no comment.

"You know," Jean went on, "Herb Bower also told me that Paul upset a few people with that factory fiasco."

That was true. More than a few folks had wanted the factory to be built, even at the risk of the environment. There were some who might hold a grudge. But, over all, Paul had come through that episode a stronger, and, in fact, more respected figure in the community. She could imagine no one who would be angry enough about his stand to attack him.

Jean sighed and stroked her son's temple. "Honey," her voice was tender, "if you'd just wake up. . . ."

Gracie couldn't stop the tears. "I wish I could do more."

"You cry with me," Jean said, softly. "That's enough."

That very night, Gracie decided at choir practice that she would get some practical nurturing organized on the Meyers' behalf. The women who kept Eternal Hope's kitchen lively for so many events also helped out with meals for new mothers, folks recuperating from illness or injury, and anyone one else who was deemed to be in need of tender loving care. Volunteers took turns delivering a family-sized meal and dessert. It felt good to have a plan to support Jean, and Gracie was eager to put it into action.

Gracie steered Fannie Mae into her usual spot in the church parking lot. Barb's car was already there. Gracie slid out and was about to lock up, when she heard her name. Barb was waving from the side entrance, her expression apprehensive.

Gracie walked over to see what was wrong.

"It's the first any of us has been in the sanctuary," Barb said, her voice trembling. "Since the accident, that is."

The accident? So no one suspected differently. Gracie was glad about that. She gave Barb's hand a squeeze and took her key. Unlocking the door was a cinch, but her stomach knotted at the thought of entering. She gave Barb a sympathetic look. They stepped over the threshold with arms locked.

"It's quiet," Barb said.

Gracie stopped to look around. The same sun as before shone through the windows; there was the same timeworn smell of vintage oak and old carpet. It felt like home to her.

Her church's sanctuary always reminded Gracie of each generation's responsibility to the next. It seemed to her that was what the Shema was all about. Abe Wasserman had made her aware of that. Deuteronomy, Chapter Six, was very special to Jewish people, so much so that they recited it every day in their prayers. The Shema, they called it—the command to pass the faith on, to tell the story of God's faithfulness.

Those verses were inscribed on parchment and nailed to Jewish door posts. Mezuzahs contained them: a scroll in a box reminding God's faithful that they were special. They had a story to tell and an obligation to tell it. A nice tradition.

Gracie turned on the lights, and Barb waited at the foot of the loft steps. "I can't stand the creaking steps."

"Think of it as a groan," Gracie told her, "an old friend waking up to be sociable." Gracie took the first step, then the second.

Er-r-r-t. She smiled. "Sounds like that friend to me."

"You're always so optimistic." Barb hit the landing and waited. "Me, I'm going to have ulcers. I worry about everything."

Gracie wanted to encourage her overanxious friend. "'Don't worry about tomorrow, for tomorrow will worry about itself.'"

Barb finished, "'Each day has enough trouble of its own. . . .' Don't I know it."

"We all let anxiety get the better of us sometimes," Gracie told her. "The important thing is to recognize it and nip it in the bud before it controls us."

Voices in the sanctuary.

Marge and Tish.

Barb excused herself and began preparing for choir practice. Gracie took her place in the alto section, only half-listening. Her attention, instead, was with the conversation Marge was having.

"*Real* men don't crochet! And don't give me the name of some athlete," Marge was telling Tish. "They just do it for attention. Rick Harding freezes garden produce, too, I heard him tell Gracie." A pause.

They were on the stairs.

"It's just not natural. A guy should do manly things like hunting and fishing, and—Gracie!" Marge smiled guiltily, much like Gooseberry with a dead critter at his feet.

"Estelle criticized the booties Marge made," Tish told her. "She said her stitches were too big, and that the babies' little toes would get pinched in the loops."

Marge crossed her arms. "It was my first pair! What did the woman expect? I haven't crocheted since . . . let's just say it's been a long time."

"Rick Harding's booties were perfect," Tish added.

A little foot stamp preceded an indignant wiggle of the hips, as Marge explained, "I just need practice." She looked at Gracie for support. "I've won Grange awards for my granny squares. Haven't I? Gracie, tell her."

She decided not to respond to Marge's plea for praise. "I'm a bit rusty, too," was all she would offer. "Maybe we get Estelle and Rick to come over to my house. Rick could give us a few pointers."

Marge's lips were tight.

Gracie was all too aware how gossip manages to betray close friends. It was one of the problems with small towns—everybody knew everyone else's business, and nobody considered choir loft prattle to be one of those Big Seven, when it was perhaps the deadliest of them all. This would have to be nipped in the bud! But was Gracie the one to do it? Marge, after all, was her very best friend.

GRACIE DUG IN HER POCKETBOOK for keys. How could a person lose a key-ring the size of a grapefruit? But they weren't in her bag. She'd had them in her hand when she saw Barb. That was right! She'd put them in her handbag to take Barb's keychain and open the door. But maybe she hadn't. They could be in the loft.

She glanced around the parking lot. Rick was talking to Barb. Marge was getting into her car. Everyone else had gone. It made sense to ask Marge to wait, so she could give her a ride if need be. After all, they were next-door neighbors. But Gracie was feeling a little annoyed with her friend. Since she was definitely interested in hearing more about Rick and Comfort's parenting arrangement, going with him might be the better choice.

Rick or Marge?

"Marge!" Perhaps she'd have the opportunity to tactfully address the subject of gossip.

Her friend hit the automatic window button. "What's the matter?"

"I've misplaced my keys—can you wait while I check inside?" There was an affirmative nod. "I'll just be a minute."

Marge unfolded herself from the driver's seat. "I'll go with you."

Gracie had to get the key from Barb again, so Rick insisted on going with them. Barb turned the lock so when they closed the door the tumbler would click. The organist was in a hurry to watch a PBS special, a Bocelli concert. Gracie remembered that Pat, the church secretary, liked Pavarotti and mentioned this to Barb, who seemed excited to discover their mutual interest in opera.

"Here I talk to her all the time, and, somehow, I didn't know," Barb said.

"You know everything about everybody," Rick told Gracie, as they walked down the aisle of the church.

Marge agreed. "The thing about her is she doesn't tell everything she knows. You can trust Gracie with your deepest, darkest secrets."

Gracie resisted the urge to make this the moment for a pointed comment about gossip. Instead, she accepted the compliment and focused on retracing her steps in hopes of finding the lost keys.

"Your booties weren't *that* bad," Rick told Marge. "Estelle was a little hard on you."

"Estelle is hard on everyone!" Marge checked the top of the organ. "She thinks she knows everything about music, just because she once had some private voice lessons. It doesn't surprise me she imagines herself equally an expert on crocheting."

She grinned sardonically. "She probably swears by Martha Stewart. Did you hear her go on about continuity? Crocheting for girls, knitting for boys. Please!"

"Marge!"

Marge exhaled, feeling behind the pew cushions. "Sorry for venting, but that woman is sooo . . ."

"Persnickety?" Rick suggested.

"Uptight," Marge said. "A big pain in the neck."

Gracie was annoyed now.

"I don't know, Gracie," Rick said, his genial manner helping to disarm her anger. "I don't think your keys are here." He stood to face her. "Maybe you better check your purse again."

Gracie's insides churned. Did he suppose she wasn't already frustrated enough with herself. "The keys are *not* in my purse!" she said, snappishly. Then feeling guilty, unfastened its clasp. "I'll check again," she amended, more meekly.

They were not in her purse.

They were not in the church.

She'd just hit the bottom step of the loft when she noticed the side entrance door ajar. Peculiar. Nobody *ever* used that door, for the very reason she'd discovered—the thing had a tendency to stick.

"What's the matter?" Rick asked, coming up behind her.

He dismissed her concern with, "Kids! They roam all over the church during the coffee hour."

"Can I give you a ride home?" Marge offered, "I'll even bring you back with the other set. Don't worry, they'll probably turn up in the daylight. We'll call Pat and have her keep a lookout."

Gracie hated feeling so off balance. This whole evening had seemed that way, and she feared she wouldn't be able to sleep that night. "Thanks, Marge," was all she could say.

Rick walked them to the car, offering to teach Marge how to knit. Gracie could tell her friend was miffed, and that she, Gracie, would get an earful in the car. Silently, Gracie wished for some of Uncle Miltie's rejected antacid tablets. She hated conflict. She hating ignoring her conscience, which was dogging her to talk to Marge. Gracie just wanted to go home to bed.

It took two glasses of warm milk and an hour's worth of a rerun of a Vienna Boys' Choir concert to calm Gracie down enough for sleep. Uncle Miltie, on the other hand, had apparently turned in early and was sleeping like a baby; his usual steady snore and whistle attested to it. Gracie washed the few dishes in the sink. The day had been unsettled and unsettling. All was not right with her world.

It would be a long night.

The next morning, Marge knocked on the kitchen window right after Uncle Miltie had left for his pinochle game at the senior center. Gracie had been hoping to get out for her prayer walk before facing her friend. She needed time alone with God. Instead, she let Marge in.

Lord, You're welcome to come in and sit a spell—have coffee with us—in fact, I wish You would. We need Your objectivity.

"Is it fresh?" Marge picked up the coffee pot in one hand and opened her cupboard door with the other. "I only have instant—thank goodness you always perc."

"Drip," Gracie corrected. Marge surely ought to have it right by now.

Marge arched a thinly tweezed eyebrow. The blue on her lids seemed excessive this morning. "It's not perc, it's *drip,*" Gracie told her. It irritated Gracie to see her friend so perfectly coiffed, and she felt ashamed. She swallowed her annoyance, and smiled. *For no matter how crusty a person appears, there's always a cream filling hiding inside.* And hadn't Marge so often proved the truth of this particular Parks family's rule!

"Drip has less acid," Gracie explained, reclaiming her hospitable nature. "It's easier on the stomach."

Marge grinned. "Tastes good, too." She took a sip, leaning

against the counter. Her gaze narrowed. "Come clean, Gracie. You're mad at me for something."

"I'm not," Gracie lied. "I didn't get much sleep. I'm angry at myself for losing those keys."

"Senior moment. We all have them, honey. They come with age. The keys are probably at the church office." Marge's expression was empathetic. "You could have dropped them in the parking lot."

"I didn't!"

Marge moved to the doorway where she could have a better view through the front window. "You sure?"

"I'm sure." Gracie craned her neck to see what her friend was looking at. "There's that car—the black convertible."

It was!

They moved closer to the window, careful to remain hidden.

"What should we do?" Marge whispered.

Gracie did the same. "Call Rocky," she answered, hardly audible even to herself.

"Not the police?"

Perhaps that was a better plan. "But what do I say? That there's man sitting in front of my house? He's not doing anything but sitting there." Then Gracie realized, "Why are we whispering?"

She picked up the phone and punched in Rocky's cell phone number and, when he answered, told him about the car.

"I'll be right there."

Marge chewed her nails and paced the living room. "Maybe we should call Herb, anyway."

"Let's wait for Rocky." Gracie began to straighten the pillows on the couch, and then it suddenly dawned on her. "I didn't put them this way."

Marge turned to face her. "*Hmm?*"

"I didn't arrange these pillows." She picked up the fat, brushed corduroy one. "This one belongs over here." She picked up the paisley from the love seat and returned it to the couch. "And this one belongs here!"

Marge shrugged. "Uncle Miltie was being helpful."

"Uncle Miltie doesn't do domestic." Her heart was racing now. "He changes fuses, fixes bad wiring, repairs rotted steps, but no pillow fluffing."

Now Marge looked scared. "Someone was here? When— during the night? While you were sleeping?"

Couldn't have been during the night. "I didn't sleep very well. Even Uncle Miltie's snoring bothered me, and that was through a couple of walls."

"So when?"

"My keys!" Panic hit. "I was locking the car door when I saw Barb. She looked scared, so I walked over to talk to her and left the keys—"

"In the door!" Marge finished her sentence. "Maybe we're not alone!" Marge's eyes grew large. "The stranger!"

Gracie put her hands up to calm Marge and took a deep breath herself. "We don't know anything about him. Let's not jump to conclusions. Uncle Miltie has been here all night. And if someone was in the house, Gooseberry would have let us know."

Then she remembered, she hadn't seen her cat this morning. But it wasn't unusual for him to stay out all night. Prowling was his hobby. "Nobody was in the house," she tried to sound convinced. "I'm pretty confident of that."

"But the pillows—the convertible—the stranger—the guy at Cordelia's!" Marge's voice was squeaky. "Gracie, I'm scared!"

Gracie reached for her friend. "The stranger we're reacting to is probably just someone passing through. Marge, there's nothing to worry about. We'll just ask the guy in that black—"

"He's gone."

Gracie followed her gaze as the vehicle disappeared from view.

Uncle Miltie arrived just ahead of Rocky, and by that time Gracie and Marge had satisfactorily searched the house. Gracie decided the prowler must have been in one of the bedrooms. She'd lived in her house long enough to know if even the air was disturbed.

Again, nothing had been taken.

"I suppose we ought to call Herb Bower," Uncle Miltie was

saying. He scratched his head. "Doesn't make sense. I was here all evening."

Gracie remembered Gooseberry and went to the back door. The furry orange creature was curled up on the mat, waiting complacently. He ambled in, as Uncle Miltie entered the kitchen.

"I thought I let him inside last night before I went to bed."

He hadn't gone out when she'd come in the night before. "Did you let him out this morning?"

"Maybe. Don't rightly remember." Uncle Miltie thought about it a minute. "Gooseberry usually prefers the back door. I went out the front."

Gracie's mind returned to the pillows. Who had trespassed in her house? She looked at Rocky and wished he was El. El would hold her tight. In his arms she wouldn't feel so afraid.

"I suppose we should call Herb, really," Rocky said, pondering the situation. "I haven't a clue how he's going handle it."

Gracie nodded, swallowing emotion. She was not going to cry.

Rocky put his arm around her. "You think the police should handle it? Or do you want me to look into it a little more?"

"Let's do it together." After all, nothing had been taken, so what could Herb, or Jim Thompson, do? Gracie trusted Rocky's journalistic instincts and her own female intuition.

She even wanted to believe it was just her imagination with regard to the pillows. Maria could have played with them. She and Doña Coca had watched television together.

On the way to the front door, Gracie looked back for a second time. She was sure she would have noticed earlier had it been Maria. Or would she? Life had gotten crazy.

Cordelia greeted them at the door of her tourist house. Giving them a sweeping invitation to enter, she eyed Rocky. "Where's the photographer?"

"Doggone it!" Rocky hit himself on the temple. "I forgot to talk to Mike Struthers about the story."

Cordelia crossed her arms. "Maybe I should cancel my subscriptions. You hear that is *plural*, Mr. Gravino?"

"I apologize, Mrs. Fountain." His eyes were pleading. "I've had a lot on my plate, what with the pastor being attacked— and now someone uninvited has been in Gracie's house!"

"Lordy be!" Cordelia's arms went around Gracie. "You poor dear!" She stepped back to check Gracie out from head to toe. "Are you okay? Were you in the house? Was anybody hurt—did he take anything? Oh, my! It doesn't bear thinking about!"

Gracie put on a positive smile. "Everyone's fine. Apparently, no one was home and nothing was taken."

"You can thank your lucky stars then!" She patted the rock-sized diamond on her left hand.

"Is Mr. Stone here?"

Cordelia shook her head. "Checked out this morning. Didn't leave a forwarding address, if that's what you're going to ask me. I didn't even check him out. Early this morning, I found the key on the front desk with a note thanking me for my hospitality."

"How did he pay?" Rocky quickly asked.

The man was sharp, Gracie gave him credit for that. She was thankful he was on top of the situation.

"Paid by cash, of course." Her smile was smug. "Those sneaky types always do. Sunglasses—dead giveaway."

They thanked her and left, but not without being reminded one more time about the story Rocky had promised the paper would do.

"We better call Herb," Gracie decided, and let Rocky dial him on the cell phone. He was waiting on the front porch with Uncle Miltie when they got there. Marge was holding Charlotte.

"Don't you have to open the shop?" Gracie debated whether to stay on the porch or invite them into the kitchen.

Marge met her gaze. "Not when my best friend needs me."

Gracie remembered again that Parks family rule—the best place to solve a problem is alone with God in a warm, cozy kitchen. That counted with friends too. Whenever two more of them gathered, God was in their midst. "Come on in!" she said, "I'll fix us a cup of coffee."

"And some of those peanutty bars," Rocky said, opening the door for her.

She smiled. "Why not?"

Gracie was happy to have Herb on her side, as he had often proved himself a stalwart ally. Nor one she knew was more fair-minded. And she knew he appreciated her, as well.

Uncle Miltie had been in the middle of one of his stories: "Like I was saying, a minister dies, see, and decked out in his clerical color and fancy robe, waits in line at the Pearly Gates. Just ahead of him is a guy dressed in jeans and Hawaiian-print shirt. Saint Peter says to this guy, 'And who are you? I need to check to see if you're on the list.' Guy tells him, he's Joe Carduci, taxi driver from Noo Yawk City. Pete smiles and tells him to grab a silk robe and golden staff. So Joe does, off he goes into heaven. The minister is next in line. Before Pete has a chance to ask the guy exclaims, 'The Reverend Horatio J. Withers, head pastor of First Church for thirty years.' Pete looks at the list and tells him to take a cotton robe and wooden staff. 'Wait a minute,' says Horatio J., 'you gave that taxi driver silk and gold, and I get wood and cotton. How can that be?'" Uncle Miltie paused at the kitchen table, apparently savoring his upcoming punch line. "'Up here, we go by results,' says Saint Pete. 'While you preached, folks slept. While Joe drove, people prayed.'"

Rocky and Herb laughed hard. Marge rolled her eyes, and Gracie was happy for a little comic relief.

They rehashed the whole case, including their theories on who was involved how. Herb took notes steadily, every once in a while asking them to repeat something.

"Now as I see it," he began, "this is what we have. Five days ago, Paul's house was gone through. The only thing missing is a cosmetic bag. Two days later, Paul is attacked in his church. Nothing was taken as far as we know. Now we have someone snooping in Gracie's place."

He turned the page. "There's a man who somehow seems to have been tagged as some kind of government investigator." He looked at Rocky, who nodded. "His name may or may not be Stone. His car was out in front of your house this morning." A glance at Gracie. "We don't know how long he was there, but Miltie doesn't remember seeing the car when he went to the senior center. So we think it was there maybe an hour, tops."

Over went another page.

Herb paused, studying his notes. "But how this Hispanic-looking stranger fellow fits in, we don't know. Abe Wasserman is the only person we know who's talked to him."

"*And* we don't know that for sure," Gracie corrected. "He's the only person *we've* talked to who's met the man. That doesn't mean others haven't."

Rocky cleared his throat. "Chuckie identified a rental car parked in front of the pastor's house."

"Alleged," Herb corrected. "He did not *identify* anything.

He told Jim a story and his friends backed him up. Jim is following up on that rental vehicle."

Gracie couldn't stop herself from commenting, "Jim could give Chuckie some slack. They boy's done nothing to incriminate himself."

It was Rocky's turn to defend Chuckie. "He's a hard-working kid who's got some typical teenage tics and twitches."

"*Hmm.* Some kids like to act out, to gain attention." Herb glanced between them. "But Jim thinks Chuckie is looking for revenge."

"With me?" Gracie found the idea incredulous.

Herb tapped his pencil on the notebook. "Got to admit, that's one snafu in the theory. But another is that it couldn't have been Chuckie last night, or this morning. The stupid kid darn near asphyxiated himself last night at the garage. He had that car running—pretty soon, it was a nightmare situation. It was after hours and things were locked up tight, not enough ventilation.

"It's a good thing Harry came back to check him or Chuckie would be a goner. They're keeping him at the hospital until at least this afternoon."

Gracie was brisk. "That settles it. I'm going to the hospital. There's nothing more we can do here anyway."

"Maybe Paul will wake up," Marge offered. "Then the mystery will be solved."

Rocky took the last gulp of coffee. "I'll take you, Gracie."

"No, you've got a paper to get out," Marge said. "I took the day off to be with my friend. Paul's our pastor. I'll take her, Rocky, if you don't mind."

Gracie feigned indignation. "Fannie Mae and I have been capable of getting everywhere on our own for a long time now."

"She's not here, dear," Marge reminded her. "She's in the church parking lot."

Gracie's heart sank. "The keys! I don't know where my keys are! The prowler could come in here any time!"

"We'll get the locks changed," Uncle Miltie said. "I'll call Roy."

Gracie decided to let herself be taken care of by her friends. Rocky said he was going to follow up on their leads, and check with Abe, as well as the other boys. Uncle Miltie was already dialing Roy Bell, the local handyman. Marge called the church, and Pat promised to look for the missing keys.

"All settled," Marge announced. "Let's go."

Gracie stopped first in her garden to pick two bouquets of flowers. Brown-eyed Susans seemed right for Chuckie. And again the daylilies reminded her of Jean, so she took them for a second time to her new friend and the sickroom where her pastor lay.

She and Marge traveled in companionable silence most of the way, but then her friend mentioned the booties.

"You know I am good at needlework," Marge told her. "It hurt my feelings that you didn't defend me last night at choir practice."

Gracie didn't want to get into it. "I was feeling kind of crusty."

"Well, you were polite enough to Rick Harding!" Marge glanced her way. "Asking him to help us like we were schoolgirls. Gracie, I have won awards! Even as a girl my handiwork was displayed in the 4-H exhibit at the county fair. I've won blue ribbons for my crocheting."

Gracie sighed. *Lord help me.* "You're very talented, Marge, but so is Rick. And you haven't done crocheting for years, you said so yourself. What you said about him to Tish was not right. Marge, it was hurtful."

"Well, I'll be!" Marge stared.

Gracie pointed. "You're going te get a red light."

A jerk to the brakes. Marge was pouting.

"So you think I was talking out of turn, being insensitive the way you'd never be?"

"Marge! Slow down!"

Another glare. "And I can't drive!"

It was not going well. They didn't say anything all the way to the hospital. As Gracie opened the door, Marge announced, "I'm going for a walk."

"In the hospital parking lot?" Gracie felt guilty.

Marge grinned ruefully. "Lawrence Family Rules to Live

By: The best place to take out your anger is on the pavement."

"I love you." Gracie reached over and squeezed her friend's hand. "Thank you for taking the day off for me."

They each started in different directions when Marge turned and called her name. "One of the blessings of having old friends is that you can afford to be stupid with them."

"Lawrence family rules?"

She shook her head. "Emerson, I think." She held out her hand. "I was stupid. Snapping at you and sniping at Rick."

"I'll walk with you."

They made a circuit around the block and returned with two wilting bunches of flowers. At the nurse's station, Gracie asked for a pair of plastic vases.

"It's amazing what a little water can do," the nurse commented, as Gracie and Marge each fussed with a bouquet.

"Amazing," Gracie agreed, thinking of a different type of water, that flowed when you most needed it.

Marge smiled. Kindred souls.

CHUCKIE SAT ON THE HOSPITAL BED flanked by two friends. They looked almost normal, except for the assorted face jewelry and body art. One young man stood and introduced himself as Quasi. Trying to ignore the ring through his nose, Gracie extended her right hand. She was impressed with his good manners, and told him as much.

The multi-pierced teenager, they called Martin. He followed suit in standing and introducing himself, but Gracie suspected that was more out of embarrassment than good manners.

"It hurts my face just looking at you," Marge said to the boy, examining the gemstone protruding from the area below his lip. Both eyebrows sported several rings apiece.

Martin shrugged, seeming not to take offense. When she

shook his hand, Gracie discovered what she thought was a bracelet was actually a tattoo. She couldn't help agreeing with Marge.

"Mrs. Parks," Quasi got her attention. "I remember you from the youth group. You helped with our snacks. You prepared the food. I remember. You're a wonderful cook."

"Thank you." Gracie scrutinized him, not recollecting any boy decorated like an aborigine on a *National Geographic* special. He must have guessed her confusion because, with much fanfare, he tucked the thing up in his nose.

"Voilà!" Quasi grinned, finally looking like any other kid in the youth group. "My grandma hates the ring, too. I don't let it show at the Willow Mart either, so I am an expert at hiding it."

She recognized him as the bagger, who also sometimes helped with carts in the parking lot. She remembered what Rocky had told her about the man in the black car and Samson, so she questioned him as to whether he had been there for the incident.

"Sure, I was there!" He laughed, turning to his friends. "You should have seen it. This little tank of a bull terrier practically broke his neck getting out the window of the car. Acted like an attack dog, so at first I thought the lady sicced the dog on the guy. The animal practically shredded the guy's pant leg. I think he drew blood."

Martin whistled. "Did they put the dog down?"

"I think there's a two-bite law," Chuckie told them.

Gracie looked at him.

"Yeah, I read it somewhere. The first bite's free, but if the dog does it again you got trouble. I thought it was funny when I read it."

Quasi laughed. "I'd believe him, Mrs. Parks, Chuck reads practically anything with words on it."

"Did you ever see that man again?"

He nodded. "Yeah, the guy came in a couple of times—bought the sandwich special and a cup of coffee. I remembered him because of the expensive sunglasses."

"He sat in his car—the car was awesome!"

"The black convertible." Marge shuddered.

"Yeah." He looked at Marge. "How did you know?"

A sheepish smile. "Seen it around."

"Anyway, the guy had to take off his coat to get rid of the dog!" Quasi broke into hysterics, barely able to continue. "The mutt yanked at his pant leg, and the guy tried to shake him off, and the dog jumped for his coat sleeve. The lady was screaming, kids were crying."

Quasi put his hand to his head. "The man pulls the jacket off with the dog hanging by his teeth. He has one of those shoulder holsters—a gun."

"Must have been a cop—maybe a narc," Martin acted like he was informing them of something. Then, turning to his friend. "You're not doing crack, are you, Quasi?"

The boys laughed, but Gracie did not appreciate their humor. She resisted the urge to lecture them. "Chuckie says you saw another car, out in front of the pastor's house."

"Yeah, we were in the park," Martin said. "I thought it was a state cop in a plain wrapper."

Gracie arched her brow perplexed.

"Unmarked car," Marge said. "Don't you watch TV, honey? They must mention them in those mysteries you devour."

She felt a little silly not recognizing the phrase. "I suppose they have," she admitted. "I'd just forgotten. Besides, it wasn't around in Miss Marple's day!"

Chuckie cut in. "The car *was* rental. Martin just gets paranoid about everything. The car was sitting there for like forever—big and dark. There was a guy in the driver's seat, so Martin thought he was maybe a narc, too."

"Yeah, that's right. The car was also a rental." Quasi sounded like he was covering. "Martin thinks there's a narc on every corner."

Martin scowled but didn't say anything.

Marge eyeballed him. "You don't have reason to worry, do you?"

"Martin's a jerk." Chuckie cut in. "Adults are suspicious enough, you don't have to go giving them more ammunition."

Gracie had more questions, but suspected they were not going to be entirely forthright, not at this time anyway.

Martin might turn out to be the weak link, however, and she would have to talk to him sometime when he was away from Chuckie and Quasi.

Before they left, she thanked them. They seemed good boys, in spite of their preoccupation with body piercing. She reckoned every generation had its conforming noncon-formists, and that it seemed to balance out as its members aged.

Gracie made sure to tell Chuckie how glad she was to see that he was okay. He bemoaned his own stupidity, saying how grateful he'd been for Harry Durant. Gracie sent a prayer on the man's behalf. Harry reminded her once again of the Parks family rule that no matter how crusty a person seems, there's always a cream filling hiding inside. She made a mental note to send Harry a card, letting him know some-one appreciated what he had done.

"I like the flowers," Chuckie said. "So will my mom." She turned to face him and he smiled, almost but not quite the first real smile from the boy that she'd ever seen. "Thank you," he mouthed.

She walked back and gave him a hug. "I've been praying for you every day," she whispered. "God loves you."

His "I feel your prayers," was barely audible.

Chuckie could not have hit Paul. Gracie was sure of it. She gave him one more hug before she left.

When they got to Paul's room a doctor was talking to

Harold. Paul's father waved them in, introducing them to Dr. Wright.

"The brain is retaining fluid," the doctor was saying. "He's got a lot of head trauma and that is unpredictable. Paul could stay unconscious for days—"

"And he might never come out," Harold finished. "Give it to me straight, Doctor. You don't have to sugarcoat the truth."

The medical man seemed to be weighing his response.

Gracie prayed silently.

"Honestly, Mr. Meyer, we just don't *know*." Dr. Wright met Harold's gaze. "There is a possibility he may not wake up, that's true. But I assure you that is not our best guess. We think he'll be fine. It's just a matter of days, I hope. Your son's pupils are dilating, and his reflexes are good. I've scheduled another scan, and then we might know a little bit more."

He put his hand on Harold's shoulder. "Just continue praying. That's the best we can do."

Gracie thanked God for such attentive care, and sensed Hal and Marge doing the same.

Marge offered to treat her to lunch in the hospital cafeteria, but Gracie's kitchen seemed more than ever the best place to be right then. Also, she'd been gone most of the morning and still didn't know about her keys. She couldn't keep her mind off the fact someone had taken them. That someone had been in her house.

That someone was him!

Gracie grabbed Marge's arm. "The guy with the gun!"

Marge gawked around the hospital foyer. "I don't see him."

"Over there, in the corner with the newspaper." The man was sitting with one leg resting on his knee. He held the sports section folded in one hand and some sort of candy bar in the other. He didn't look so threatening.

"I say we confront him," Marge whispered. "Catch him off guard before he has a chance to slip away. We'll act nonchalant, tell him we remember him from church."

They stopped at their vantage point beside a large potted palm. "He's actually not that tall," Marge said. "And balding. Chomping that candy bar doesn't help." Marge groaned. "I can't believe I thought he looked distinguished. Looks more like a traveling salesman than an undercover agent."

"Marge!"

"I can imagine, can't I?" She put her hands on her hips. "I figured if we were going to have some federal representative, we might as well make him big-time. Besides, Department of Highway guys don't carry guns."

Marge took the first steps toward the fellow. "Let's go." She turned around when Gracie hesitated. "Well, are we going to confront him or not?"

The man must have heard Marge, because he was on his feet. He put the newspaper on the next chair and the candy bar in his coat pocket. "Ma'am. Mrs. Parks?"

"How do you know me?" Gracie wanted to know.

Before the man had a chance to answer, Marge was in his face. "Don't act innocent! We saw your car out in front of her house. We know who you are."

"Pardon me?"

"Taking our taxpayers' money to do Peeping Tom numbers on small-town widows!" Marge put her hands on her hips still glaring. "What's the CIA coming to?"

He took her gently by the elbow, signaling her to drop her voice. "Ma'am, I don't know who you *think* I am, but I am not in the CIA. And you're making a scene."

He glanced around. Gracie followed his gaze. The woman at the desk was watching and so were several of the others lounging in the reception area. "Marge, let's walk outside."

"Good idea," he said.

"Not so fast, *buster*," Marge demanded, at least keeping her voice lowered. "I want to see some ID first. I want to know just whom we're dealing with. Snooping around my friend's house is not nice—not nice at all!"

He allowed himself a moment of exasperation. "Lady, you're worse than that bull terrier."

Marge didn't bat an eye. "Identification, please!"

"All right." He slipped his hand between the jacket and his chest.

"You pull a gun and I'll scream."

This was going too far. Gracie pulled on Marge's arm,

trying to make sure she noticed Gracie giving her the eyebrow treatment.

"Calm down, lady. Here's my identification." He flipped it open, and Marge squinted to read it.

Gracie peered over Marge's shoulder. *Bruce Stone, Immigration and Naturalization Service.*

"Immigration!" Both women said at once.

Marge was clearly humiliated, but Gracie felt relieved. At least this wasn't espionage or something worse. But the INS? "I've never even been out of the country."

With a flip of his wrist, Stone closed the trifold and put it back in his jacket pocket. Marge suddenly seemed three inches shorter. She took a step back, still watching him. "He *could* have been CIA," she muttered.

Stone apologized, formally introducing himself. Gracie did the same and introduced Marge "The Human Bull Terrier" Lawrence, her best friend. They made small talk for a couple of minutes, Gracie telling him they'd heard about the Samson debacle.

"Why are you following her?" asked an only slightly chastened Marge. "And why were you in front of her house this morning?"

They were on the hospital steps. "I'll walk you to your car." He looked at Gracie. "You were leaving?" She nodded and pointed the direction of Marge's car. The silver Taurus had rainbow streamers for easy identification.

On the way to their cars Stone detailed the case. He was looking for Vincente Juarez. The man had not been convicted of any crimes, but was suspected as an accomplice in a high-profile international scandal. "I am not at liberty to discuss the case, since it involves American interests."

"American interests?" Marge was wide-eyed.

Stone eyed her. "Let me assure you, Mrs. Lawrence, it is not espionage, money laundering or anything else that sensational. Juarez may have information that can be helpful to both governments in untangling a messy, and possibly embarrassing, situation for both countries."

"So why talk to me?" Gracie wanted to know.

Stone stood by his car. "We thought he'd lead us to bigger fish, so I've been following him. The man's the brother of Cleo Vidal—Maria's mother. I didn't know how close they were, but then he turned up here. I wasn't following you—I was trying to pick up a lead on him."

"He was in my house?"

"I thought as much."

Marge was indignant again. "You thought as much? You didn't know? Why didn't you arrest him?"

He gave a helpless shrug. "We really want to know with whom he's involved. I hate to admit it . . . I lost him."

"You lost him?"

Stone nodded. "At O'Hare. Luckily he rented a car—that's

what lead me here. Your police department ran a plate check on a deserted vehicle and it turned out to be the rental. My department forwarded that information to me, and I came here. I suspect he knows I was tailing him.

"I've been checking around for a couple of days, not wanting to tip my hand. I've seen the car, but not him. It was on the other side of the street from your house a few nights ago. I snooped around and that's when I met that beast for the first time. I high-tailed it out of the alley."

Gracie remembered the barking. It was the night she had had the Meyers to her house for supper.

"So you don't know where he is?" Marge asked. "This is a *small* town."

He shook his head.

"Okay, why church?" Marge's gaze was uncompromising. "Surely you didn't think the guy would go to Sunday school."

"I went to church for me. I chose yours because of the Meyers. I just wanted to check them out, get a feel for whether they could be involved."

The man seemed to be telling them the truth. Gracie felt a little guilty for judging him so harshly. "And?" She wanted to know what he thought about the family.

"They seem to be just who they appear to be— missionaries."

At first, Stone thought Juarez might have some emotional connection to Maria, and had stopped in Willow Bend to visit his niece. Cordelia Fountain had unwittingly filled him in on the break-in at the pastor's house and the attack, so Stone had suspected Juarez was looking for something. Gracie had a hunch the man from the INS knew what that something was, and just wasn't telling.

"My office called this morning," he said. "The rental car was returned. I remembered Juarez's departing flight was scheduled for the day after tomorrow. So I decided to head back to Chicago to wait him out."

He looked at Gracie. "I dropped by your place on impulse. Mrs. Fountain told me you were close to the Meyers—and that you have a reputation for being a bit of a sleuth. 'Our Jessica Fletcher,' she called you."

"But why talk to me?"

"I was headed back to Chicago with nothing. I was going to have to intercept Juarez on a hunch—no evidence. He came to the States for a reason. If we get some proof . . . find out he's made contact with one of the other suspects—but I have nothing. I don't even have a suspect anymore.

"I just wanted to pick your brain. It was in front of your house that I got the word a motel owner called in the rental as an abandoned vehicle. The place was out at the highway exit. So I changed my mind about talking to you. Figured I'd talk to the owner and see what he knew."

His story seemed to make sense. But if he hadn't been in her house then it had to have been Maria's uncle. Gracie was more curious, and about to ask Stone about that, when he continued.

"I stopped at the hospital to check on your pastor, hoping he may have regained consciousness. I suspect it was Juarez who knocked him out, but I have no motive. I saw you ladies come in, and decided to wait until you left."

He eyed Marge. "Then you steamrolled me."

"I am sorry," Marge confessed. "We were really upset about someone going in Gracie's house. The someone could have been you. We don't know you from Adam. You *could* have been CIA."

He chuckled. "Not likely. This isn't Miami, lady."

Marge slipped her arm through Gracie's. "So who do you think was in Gracie's house? Was it Juarez? Is she in any danger?"

"I don't know. I'm not even sure it *was* Vincente in her house. I'm not really sure of anything, except that the Meyers are probably connected. My guess is that it involves the kid."

Gracie filled him in on the case, telling him about the missing cosmetic case, and how someone had taken her keys at the church the night before and had used them to search her house.

"Then your prowler might not be Juarez. I think he's already gotten what he wanted, with someone then picking him up. He found what he was looking for and headed back to Chicago. It's not uncommon for a guy like him just to leave the rental parked somewhere."

"Or he could still be in town," Gracie theorized, "and he's switched vehicles. I'm almost convinced someone was in my house last night."

"No offense intended, Mrs. Parks, but *almost* only counts in horse shoes and hand grenades. Misplaced pillows are hardly concrete evidence. And you said your uncle was in the house."

Someone had been in the house! But Gracie realized there was no sense in trying to convince him of the fact.

Stone gave Gracie his cell phone number, telling her to call if she learned anything more. "I'm going to stick around another day. That is, if I can get my room back with Mrs. Fountain."

Gracie told him about Rocky and the feature story, encouraging him to be charming. "And don't wear the sunglasses!" she called from Marge's car.

The church secretary still had not turned up the keys, so they used the spares.

Rocky was on Gracie's front stoop when she arrived home. Uncle Miltie was in the glider. Marge parked her car and joined them.

When Rocky scowled, his bushy eyebrows and dark eyes were pretty intimidating. Gracie felt herself apologizing almost before he said anything. Marge cut in, spewing out the whole story. Of course, her version turned out to be more dramatic, more cliff-hanging and more satisfyingly tidy than real life.

Uncle Miltie's eyes were as big as saucers. Marge was in her glory! Gracie couldn't help thinking, *birds of a feather.*

"Bruce Stone?" Rocky pulled his cell phone. "Let's see what I can come up with on him.

"Yeah, S-t-o-n-e, Bruce, INS, see what you can turn up. Call me at Gracie's. That's right, number one."

"What's number one?" Marge wanted to know.

There was the merest hint of a blush.

"Gracie's number!" Her friend guessed. "Gracie's telephone number is the first one on your automatic dial, right? Did you hear that, Gracie?"

"How about lunch?" was all their hostess could think to say.

Rocky covered his embarrassment by bounding up the stairs and reaching for the door before her. "Ladies?" A chivalrous sweep of his arm. Marge just couldn't resist winking.

Gracie retrieved the lettuce, tomatoes and turkey from the refrigerator, and paused to listen to Rocky recapitulate what had transpired.

"So do you think Juarez got what he wanted and left?" she asked her friend.

"Doesn't explain someone snooping around your house." Rocky leaned against the counter beside her. "Or why he'd hit Paul."

Marge set the table. "Unless the cases aren't related, but it does seem too coincidental for them not to be."

"Can I help with anything, Gracie?" Rocky asked.

She shook her head. "You can get the chips." She pointed to the cupboard. "Top shelf—out of temptation's way."

"Those guys like Stone don't divulge anything they don't have to." Marge put the place mats on the table. "There still may be more to this that he's keeping to himself."

Uncle Miltie lifted his elbows so she could set out the mat. "How do you know?"

"Don't you watch TV?"

"*Hmph!*" Uncle Miltie looked to Rocky. "You know this guy being with the INS could be a cover. Of course, that wouldn't be a Hollywood-type choice. But what do we know about him, anyway?"

"Mr. Stone? He seemed honest to me," Gracie confessed. "There was something likable about the man, I can't tell exactly what it is, but I know there was. Besides, he goes to church."

Rocky reached for the bag. "Well that cinches it! The guy's a saint."

"It's a strange case," Gracie said, choosing to ignore Rocky's sarcasm. "It is all coincidence. I don't like missing pieces. I hate when things don't add up." She chuckled, thinking, *That's why I probably hate balancing the checkbook.*

Her listeners agreed.

"If things added up, it wouldn't be mystery," Uncle Miltie announced. "Why, then you'd have a solution." He toyed with the salt shaker Marge had just put on the table. "The case would be closed and we wouldn't be having this discussion."

Marge put her hands on her hips. "What's your point, George Morgan, or are you just blowing hot wind?"

"I'm saying, facts are facts. We just aren't seeing them from the right angle, that's all. There isn't any such thing as coincidence: everything happens for a reason."

Gracie stopped slicing tomatoes. "I suspect this to be one big tapestry. We just haven't yet pulled the common thread."

"Or piece of yarn." Marge looked at her, expecting her to acknowledge the play on words. "Common thread or not, we could end up tearing apart a perfectly usable pair of booties!"

She shook her head, indicating to Marge that she'd gotten the message. Her friend was still a bit miffed at Estelle for unraveling her inferior booties.

Gracie decided her uncle was on to something. She glanced at him and said to the others, "Sometimes it doesn't seem to matter what the facts are, it only seems to matter what the people *think* the facts are. We blamed Chuckie for the break-in. We suspected him of hitting Paul. He seemed the most likely suspect, but I don't think he did it, either. That a family of missionaries can be involved in international intrigue seems far-fetched, but it is beginning to look like they are."

"We can't prove this Juarez fellow is connected to the Meyers," Rocky pointed out.

It dawned on Gracie. "Wait a minute! Stone told us as much—Maria is his niece! He was here because of her! He has no other connections. So he's either gotten what he wants, perhaps the cosmetic bag, or he's still looking for something that he thinks I might have."

"What would you have?" Marge asked.

Gracie shook her head. "I've asked myself that, and couldn't come up with anything."

"Unless he thinks the Meyers gave it to you, but that would involve them." Rocky looked at her. "And you're sure they are who they seem. I hate to burst your Pollyanna bubble, Gracie, but churched is not a synonym for innocence."

"I know that." She was feeling a bit defensive and wanted to be able to return Rocky's cynicism with a softer, more positive attitude. She held his gaze a moment, contemplating the best response.

Rocky let loose a guffaw.

Everyone else was staring, but she just flashed him a conciliatory smile.

"What, what, what?" Uncle Miltie demanded. "Come on, what's so funny?"

Rocky shook his head. "Gracie as a judge of character."

Then Uncle Miltie hit the fork on the table. "We've got to find that uncle of Maria's. Nobody at the senior center has seen a Spanish fellow."

"Uncle Miltie!" Gracie was worried what he might have let slip.

He second-guessed her. "I was discreet."

"Well, he's also not staying with Cordelia Fountain," Gracie reminded them.

Rocky jolted at the sound of her name. "I forgot to mention. She's going to be featured front and center in the Weekend edition."

"She won't have to cancel all those subscriptions." Gracie smiled at Rocky.

He laughed. "And my paper won't go broke!"

"But best of all," she reminded him, "you've made a friend for life. Cordelia really is the dearest biddy."

He snorted. "The woman's singleminded, that's for sure."

"Got to love her though," Gracie reminded him. "She's a keen judge of character."

"Sunglasses! Block the eyes, right."

Now Uncle Miltie was confused again.

"Long story." Rocky groaned, and sat down.

They hadn't finished their lunch when the phone rang.

"Gracie, Jim Thompson here. I have the Moon kid under arrest. He says he wants to see you."

She couldn't believe she'd heard right. "I just left him at the hospital."

"Let him out this afternoon. I was there when he was discharged. He's eighteen, you know—legally an adult. It's a serious crime hitting a police officer. Lucky punch—almost busted my jaw, though."

Another prayer went heavenward. "I'll be right there!"

"What's going on?" Rocky asked for the rest of the lunch party.

She took a deep breath. What else could go wrong now? "Chuckie Moon punched Jim Thompson. He's down at the jail. I've got to go, he's asking for me."

"I'll go with you." Rocky was out of the chair.

Thank goodness Jim hadn't put the boy in a cell. Herb Bower was there when she and Rocky arrived. Jim's cheek was swollen, but he actually seemed in a good humor—all things considered.

"You want to tell Mrs. Parks what happened?" Herb prodded the teenager. Gracie noticed his voice was kind.

Chuckie kept his head lowered. "She can see. Besides, Thompson already told her what happened."

"I don't want to press charges, Mrs. Parks," Jim interjected. "But Chuckie is forcing me. He wants to go to jail, said as much. That's why I called you. Maybe you can talk some sense into the kid."

Gracie took the chair beside the boy. "Suppose you explain what happened. Tell me your side of the story."

"I did what I swore I wouldn't do."

A dull stare. Was Chuckie measuring her reaction? He didn't convey a glimmer of emotion. She closed her eyes to pray for both wisdom and forbearance, as Chuckie told her what happened.

Jim Thompson had arrived at the hospital just as Chuckie was checking out. His friends were standing nearby, and Jim had made comments about their jewelry before questioning Chuckie. The boy felt like he was being interrogated, backed into a corner.

Chuckie explained he had actually started to feel claustrophobic, and couldn't breathe. Jim kept poking him in the shoulder, saying he'd better come clean before the pastor fingered him. Chuckie asked him to back off, but Jim had kept on pressing. Gracie could easily picture the scene.

"Then I hauled off and punched him. I wasn't thinking straight. It was like a volcano inside of me erupting." The boy was practically crying. "And I promised myself I would never get that mad again."

Chuckie covered his face with his hands. "But I did—I did what I swore I wouldn't. I deserve to do time. Some kind of punishment."

Grace touched his shoulder. "So you blew it, okay? Everybody does from time to time. Now you just tell Officer Thompson how sorry you are, and try again. He's has already forgiven you—he's said as much. It's time to forgive yourself."

"That's right, kid," Rocky said, standing behind Gracie.

Chuckie kept his head lowered. "But I deserve jail."

"Yes, you do." Jim sat on the edge of the desk next to him.

Gracie wanted to interrupt, but Jim went on, "I deserve reprimanding, too. The chief can write me up—put me on probation."

Herb leaned back in seat, glancing between the two of them. "You're right, Jim, you crossed the line. You interrogated the boy, embarrassed him in front of his friends and the hospital staff. And you, Charles, hit a police officer. Both are serious charges."

"I'm sorry," Jim said to Herb. "I betrayed my badge. Then he looked at Chuckie, his expression sad. "You hit me in the jaw, but it was my heart that took the punch harder. I realized I'd pushed a kid over the edge. That wasn't very mature."

He offered Chuckie his right hand. "Will you forgive me?"

"I—guess so." Chuckie looked at him through downturned eyes. "I shouldn't have hit you, though. I was giving you a hard time. You were just doing your job."

Jim put a hand on his shoulder. "We were both in the wrong."

"I do try to keep my cool," Chuckie assured him. "I mean to keep a lid on my temper, but then I go and blow it."

"So you fall down," Rocky told him, "we all do. You have to pick yourself back up. Learn from your mistakes."

Jim agreed. "I'm going to see your shocked face anytime I turn tough on a kid, and I'll remember what I pushed you to do."

Chuckie shook his head. "Yeah, but I was to blame. I rub everybody the wrong way. My temper gets the better of me. I fall down *a lot!*"

Gracie met his gaze. "You fall down seven times, you stand up eight. That takes courage, Chuckie. And I know you are a brave boy."

"Acknowledging mistakes is the beginning of conquering them," Rocky told him.

Gracie finished. "And the beginning of wisdom. Wisdom will keep you from losing your temper."

"I thought the fear of the Lord was the beginning of wisdom," Rocky said, smiling.

She chuckled, realizing he was baiting her, letting her know once again that he was familiar with the Bible. "That, too. The fear of the Lord *is* the prerequisite. Meaning it isn't remorse, or fear of humiliation or punishment that prompts us to do what is right, but fear of disappointing God."

Jim nodded. "God is generous. He forgives us time and time again. He's the God of the second chance."

"And the third and fourth?" Chuckie wanted to know.

"Through the four hundred and ninetieth," Gracie told him. "And then some."

She put her arm around him. "God's mercy is unfathomable."

13

GRACIE SLIPPED HER NEW KEY in the lock, and shivered for a second, remembering that her home had been violated. She'd lived in this house for most of her adult life and had never worried about anything. She, like Paul, had forgotten to lock her back door on many occasions. It had never concerned her, but now turning the key was cause for dread.

Oh, Lord, You are the guardian of my house and my soul.

She opened the front door as the mantle clock chimed six o'clock. *It feels a lot later.* It had been a long day, and her body ached, and once again, she was going to have to struggle to sleep. Tonight would be worse yet, knowing how vulnerable her little household really was.

The living room lamp was dimmed; Uncle Miltie was asleep in his favorite chair. Gracie turned off the television and sat down on the couch. The answering machine on the table beside her was blinking. Four messages.

She hit the button. The first was from Chuckie, "Hey, Mrs. Parks—just wanted to say thanks. Thanks for being there today—and for praying for me."

She closed her eyes and lifted the troubled teenager to God, thanking Him for surrounding the boy with good people. She sensed Chuckie had gained advocates in Jim, Herb and Rocky. There was something about becoming vulnerable that seemed to tender friendship. Men needed friendship as much as women—particularly teenaged boys.

Lord, draw Chuckie close. Let him see Your generous heart, experience Your acceptance and love.

She hit "Play." The second message was from Barb Jennings. She'd found a perfect cantata for the consecration service for the Honduras project. Barb was excited that the Latin piece utilized castanets and maracas, and wanted Gracie to accompany with one or the other.

Gracie did a little cha-cha-cha movement with her shoulders, hands in the air. She loved the Latin beat almost as much as jazz, and jazz almost as much as good old-fashioned Southern gospel. And Southern gospel just about as much as sacred arias. As she thought about it, she realized she just plain loved music!

The third call was from Estelle, checking to see how she was doing with the booties. The woman was already finishing her ninth pair. Gracie made a mental note to hunt up her knitting needles, and to buy some soft, variegated pastel yarn.

"I love you, Mom." It was Arlen. She hit the button again, savoring those opening words. "Wendy took me to look at the studio—it's small, but workable. There's a big window seat. Elmo curled up with his favorite picture book while we measured for the practice bar and mirrors. It's going to work, Mom. Thanks for praying."

Gracie smiled. *Thank You again, Lord!*

She decided the next day she'd look for a studio-warming gift. It would take her mind off the current situation. Marge would have a good suggestion; she might even have something novel in that shop of hers. She utilized every nook and cranny for an array of gifts, from picture frames to bric-a-brac to candles and soaps.

It was time she went to visit Arlen and his family. She'd been meaning to, then gotten overwhelmed with the church, catering and friends. Besides, she hadn't wanted to do it alone. But she wouldn't be alone. She smiled at that recognition. "You'll go with me, won't You, Lord?"

You will be with me. You will never leave me or forsake me.

She could take Fannie Mae, drive to Chicago, and see her niece Carter, then take a train to New York. That would be fun. Or she could fly! She'd always wanted to do that.

She would discuss these ideas with Arlen and Carter.

Thoughts of her loving family had supplanted distress, and for that, she was also thankful.

Uncle Miltie stirred.

"Mer-oww." It was Gooseberry sitting at her feet. She coaxed him to her lap and stroked his warm stripey pumpkin fur. No, she was not alone. She had the best company.

"Cat wants out." Uncle Miltie mumbled, half asleep.

"Have a nice nap?"

His eyes were slits. "What time is it?"

"A little after six."

He reached for the remote control. "What happened to my program? I missed the ending. You want to watch something else with me? Maybe a Poirot or a *Murder She Wrote* rerun?"

"Anything but a mystery!" Her nerves had been chafed enough for one day. She was feeling content and didn't really want to think. There was something about an pet that engendered peace. Gooseberry looked up, enjoying the attention. Gracie cooed feline endearments, and said to Uncle Miltie, "Pick something light, a comedy perhaps."

He flicked through the channels.

"Did you eat?"

"Warmed up the chicken," he said. "How did it go with the Moon boy?"

"Jim didn't press charges. I think Chuckie was as upset over what he did as Jim was, maybe even more so. Anyway, now things are much better between the two of them.

Chuckie had that chip on his shoulder sanded down a bit. I think Jim learned a lesson, too."

"Yeah, if he's going to bully, he better learn to dodge the punches."

Gracie shook her head. "Uncle Miltie!"

"I call a spade a spade. Jim Thompson's a good guy, but has a bit too much badge for his chest."

She let that remark pass.

"I was afraid I was going to nod off, so I put the answering machine on. Before I did, though, that friend of Rocky's, who was going to do the digging on Stone, called back."

"And?" Gracie said, very curious to know what had been learned. "How did you get him to tell *you* anything?"

"Oh," Uncle Miltie said, with one of his winks, "I just reminded him of my couple of prizes for investigative reporting. And I told him Rocky never made a move without me."

Gracie just laughed.

"Anyway, he said Stone is just who he says he is," Uncle Miltie said. "Seems that that politician Maria's mom worked for may have been taking bribes. Some big company was pushing the government to appropriate rainforest land. Guess it's mostly pristine and home to an indigenous tribe. He said the case also involves American politicians. Hot stuff."

She couldn't resist saying, "We're *all* Americans, Uncle Miltie. Honduras is in Central America."

"Touché! I'll have to remember that one." He chuckled.

"Can't figure how the Meyers or Maria figure in, though. I've been sitting here pondering. You think that guy might be trying to extort money—threaten Harold and Jean with taking back Maria?"

"What would he be looking for?" She asked, mulling over this last, dreadful possibility. "Why go through the houses? Why hit Paul?"

"Maybe he was looking for documents. Maria said her mother worked for rich people, and that they were very generous. Maybe they left her some kind of bonds."

Gracie gave that some thought. "Jean hasn't mentioned it. But Rocky is coming by in the morning. We're going to that motel where they found the rental car. I'll discuss it with him on the way out to the highway."

"Sounds like a logical lead," Uncle Miltie told her. "What about Mr. Stone? He's probably already checked."

"Rocky's going to phone him. He'll call back with any changes in the plans." She rubbed Gooseberry's chin. She didn't want to think about that, not now.

The drive to the interstate connection was companionable. She and Rocky chatted about the *Gazette*. She told him how much she liked the paper's recent change of design. In spite of what Cordelia Fountain thought, the paper regularly featured lots of local color, and Rocky, as editor, had long ago become attuned to small-town ways.

"You feature the owner of the place, he buys more advertising. That's just plain common sense, Gracie. Advertising runs the world. The challenge is in the balancing act."

"You do a fine job!"

"Thank you, my dear."

They switched to local politics, and she complimented him on his recent editorial on the county's Blue Laws. Though not a supporter, he had listened to his fellow townspeople who were, and he had written fairmindedly. El would have approved, she told him, finally getting around to talking about her husband, whom Rocky had always respected—and vice-versa—even when their views differed.

Like Rocky, her husband always had stood his ground. That was the reason he had run for mayor and served two terms; he would rather have been fishing. "If you're going to make yourself the bull's-eye," El was fond of saying, "then you have to expect to get the arrows." As mayor of Willow Bend, he had won the admiration of all, even those with their bows at the ready.

Oh, how I miss that man!

Gracie sighed, feeling that Rocky understood her sadness. After all, Rocky had been widowed, too. "How long before it stops hurting so much to remember?"

He didn't answer her until they pulled into the motel parking lot. There, he turned in his seat and met her gaze.

"On holidays, at favorite places, or during special moments, the pain is still strong. But it becomes more . . . bittersweet . . . with time." He forced a smile. "Gracie, memories become good company, like aged wine."

"I'm afraid if they were wine, I'd be drunk most of the time." Gracie looked away, feeling a little guilty for being so candid. "I worry that I think about him too much of the time. Practically everything reminds me of El."

He squeezed her hand. "That's to be expected. You had a long, happy marriage. Most of your prized memories involve him. Of *course*, you're going to remember! Gracie, you've got a new life now. El would be proud of you. I don't think what you feel is unhealthy at all. Your feelings are perfectly natural for a woman who loved her husband so much. I see the way you look out for new widows. I'm not much for religion, but if God really does use tragedy, he used El's greatly."

"Thank you." She squeezed his hand in return.

Thank You, Lord, for good friends.

The owner of the motel greeted them, and they asked about Vincente Juarez. Few foreigners passed through here, and there had also been the situation with the abandoned rental car. "He paid his bill with cash. Stayed two nights. He even left the receipt for the rental car. Weirdest thing."

It figured that he would use cash. He couldn't be traced. Gracie stared at the signature on the rental agreement. He'd paid cash in advance. But Juarez didn't use an alias. Then she remembered Stone telling her that he had a round-trip plane ticket. That didn't sound like a criminal. It stood to reason then, that he did not expect to be followed. Had he discovered Stone was, in fact, following him? Could he really have left town?

Maybe Uncle Miltie was right with his extortion theory. The man could have discovered that the Meyers had nothing. After all, Jean said her engagement ring was the only thing she possessed that had any real value. That didn't satisfy Gracie, however. She still had a hunch there was something more.

"You don't know anything about him?" Rocky was asking.

The owner shrugged. "He made a lot of long-distance phone calls to the same number. I told the state police as much. I don't think he's wanted for anything. They had the car picked up, and that's all I heard, until you two showed up. Why is it you're looking for him, anyway?"

Rocky was busy writing down the number on the phone register. "I suppose he paid cash for his phone bill," Gracie thought out loud.

"Yep. I just added it to the room bill." The man looked right at Gracie. "What did you say your interest is in this guy?"

Gracie searched her brain for something discreet. "We're friends of his niece. We think he's trying to find her." She hated being evasive, but it was better than out-and-out lying.

"The girl's family were all killed in the monster storm

that hit Honduras. Vincente Juarez may be her only living relative."

That was the truth.

The telephone number turned out to be for an office in Virginia. Gracie called Stone with the information, and he made that confirmation. Stone had checked the nearby restaurants and convenience stores. No one remembered Juarez; he appeared to be invisible. Or so it seemed—after all, he had slipped into her house without Uncle Miltie suspecting.

Rocky dropped Gracie off at her house. Since Rick Harding's car was sitting in Marge's driveway, Gracie walked over to see her friends. Charlotte met her at the back door with an anything-but-ferocious *yip-yip-yip*. Rick was already sitting at her kitchen table.

"Knit one, purl two," he greeted. "Margie can knit!"

"Margie?" She shot an incredulous look at her friend.

Marge grinned sheepishly. "Makes me feel younger."

"She told me that all of her friends used to call her that," Rick said. "I've been having a good time with her." He winked. "Doesn't she look like a Margie?"

"No!" both women said in unison.

Rick's expression was crestfallen.

They all laughed.

"I was humoring you, honey," Marge told him. She winked back at him. "Truth be known, I do kind of like the nickname."

At another moment, Marge might have had hysterics upon hearing this variation of her name. Gracie knew it was what her high-school friends had called her, but no one else after that had ever dared. She hadn't even allowed her husbands to call her that. Rick obviously had charmed her.

Gracie looked at what almost resembled a bootie. "You've really learned to knit!"

"I told her she could it!" Rick said. "You know, she's won prizes for her crocheting? For someone that talented, switching to knitting needles is a breeze."

Gracie thought Marge blushed, covering it by turning to her Shih Tzu. "See, Charlotte, you *can* teach an old dog new tricks."

"How about this old lady," Gracie said, pulling out a chair. "You have needles and yarn for her?"

Rick scrambled to get his bag out from under the table. "We have twenty pairs of booties already," he told her, retrieving a pair of knitting needles. "Estelle checked with everyone. We're going to bring them to our formal meeting. Then we'll make up a few layettes to put in a bassinet."

"Marybeth suggested that," Marge said. "She has one in the attic—wicker. I told her you and I would decorate with a Spanish flair. I've got some scarves and things at the store we can use."

Rick handed her a skein of the variegated yarn Gracie had intended to purchase. "They were having a good sale, so I bought ten of these."

"Just the color I was going to buy!" She picked up a set of knitting needles and started to work. Rick continued to offer help in his low-key way. Gracie relaxed, letting friendly chatter and clicking needles carry her away, once again thankful for friends.

"Blessing upon blessing," she praised God out loud.

Marge looked her way. *"Hmm."*

"God's best gifts He wraps in flesh!"

"Blessing upon blessing," they agreed.

Gracie stopped at the hospital later that afternoon. On her way to Paul's room, she dialed Mr. Stone on her cell phone. "Did you get your room back?"

"Not until I played twenty questions with Mrs. Fountain," Stone told her. "She's almost as scary as your pit bull friend, Mrs. Lawrence. Since I'd left, before, she'd somehow become convinced I was up to no good."

Gracie chuckled. "Sunglasses."

"She said something about them, told me I need to look at people when I speak."

"Eye contact is important to some people."

Mr. Stone concurred. "It's important to me, too! That's how I judge honesty. That's probably why I avoid it. Occupational hazard. I've never been comfortable with deception of any kind. I probably shouldn't have taken this promotion.

"I used to be a paper shuffler, but wanted a bit more

excitement. I think they call it the Peter Principle—you're promoted to your level of incompetence. That's me, the bungling investigator. I lost Juarez, after all."

Gracie felt sorry for the man, and tried to be encouraging. He updated her on his search for Maria's relative. The man had called to confirm his flight, using the pay phone at the Willow Mart. In less than forty-eight hours, he would be on a plane to Honduras.

What could he have been looking for?

Harold and Maria were sitting bedside vigil. Maria had crayoned and pinned up masterpieces: scenes of her native Honduras, a nostalgically appealing picture of a fat orange cat, and one of a dark-haired girl standing in the middle of a smiling blond family of four.

Harold offered her his seat, telling Gracie at the same time that not much had changed. But Paul was at least stirring every now and again. Though regaining consciousness for longer periods, he still was groggy.

"I pray for my brother," Maria said softly.

Harold walked to the window, and staring out, said, "It's tough, tougher than I'd thought, to let go of a child. He's in God's hands. And we have hope—always hope."

Gracie walked to put her hands on his shoulders. "Sometimes day by day and minute by minute."

"He's going to be okay." Harold kept his gaze fixed outside while reaching for her hand. "We've gained so many friends, felt so much love. Something good is going to come out of this, I know it."

He turned around and smiled, propping himself on the radiator and telling her to sit down. She sat down next to Maria and watched her finish what appeared to be a self-portrait.

"You're quite an artist," Gracie told her.

Maria handed her the picture. "For you."

"Oh, thank you! I'll hang it on my refrigerator—the place of honor. My favorite art gallery."

Maria started another picture, and Gracie studied the sober face of a little girl in the one given to her. Doña Coca smiled at her from the paper. "She is a beautiful lady." Gracie pointed to the rendition of the doll. "She's a very special friend, and it shows in your artwork."

"My best friend."

"You've been through a lot together, haven't you?"

A quick nod.

Gracie tried to think of a tactful way to question Maria about her knowledge of her uncle. She could not come up with a way to do it gently, so she changed direction. "How long have you had Doña Coca?"

"A very long time." A doe-eyed smile. "*Abuelita* made her for me. She said I needed a grandma to watch out for me when she could not be there. My mother's family are *campesinos*—farmers. We lived in the *barrio* outside the city. They have a small plot of land. The money was never enough for our large family. Mama took the job in Tegucigalpa to help."

Gracie fussed with the doll, which now sat on Paul's bed tray. She straightened and smoothed the brightly colored circle skirt, feeling a twinge of heart-sickness. "I don't get to see my grandson nearly enough." She looked at Maria. "I miss him a lot. I bet your grandmother missed you, too."

"We went home every Saturday. I stayed in the big house so I could go to school. As I told you, it was there I learned English. Sometimes we took the bus, but sometimes my uncle would come. Tío Vincente worked in the city, also."

Vincente! She knew the man! Gracie glanced at Harold, wondering if he had talked to his wife about the possibility of Juarez being involved, but his expression was inscrutable.

"Tell me about your uncle," she coaxed. "Was he special?"

Harold stood. "Cleo's youngest brother. Maria's mother was his sister."

She hated bringing it up. "He didn't die?"

"No." Harold paused, perhaps uncomfortable about talking about the man in front of Maria. "Our pastor tried to find him for Maria's sake."

He looked at the girl, and Gracie followed his gaze. Maria pressed the blue crayon against the paper, fiercely coloring a skyscape. Gracie was instantly sorry she'd asked the question. She stroked the child's back.

"Tío Vincente was nice to me. He had a car and came to get us sometimes. He and Mama would argue in quiet voices. I knew his work did not please her. My grandparents were often angry with him, too, so he did not come home with us often."

She looked at Harold. "My papa is right in saying that my uncle did not care what happened to me. Tío Vincente had a life for which he was ashamed. I could tell by the tone he used with *Abuelita* and Mama. He used it with me, too, always wanting me to understand how important it was to earn money—to make a better life. He wanted to help my grandparents. I know they would not take his help and that made him sad."

She turned to Gracie. "But do not be sad for me. My *abuelita* says that baptism water is thicker than blood. Now, I have family, that is what matters. *Familia.*" She smiled at Harold again. "My uncle is my uncle, I did not choose him. *Don* Harold and *Doña* Jean are my parents. I chose them for my Papa and Mama. And my brother Paul, too."

Gracie felt herself choking up. Harold brushed some tears from his cheeks and bent over to hug his little girl.

GRACIE WAS ON HER WAY to Abe's Deli when Chuckie Moon darted across the street to intercept her. He doubled over panting. "I—ran all the way—from the park."

She put her hand on his shoulder. "Take it easy. Whatever it is will hold until you get your breath."

He took a few strong gulps of air, nodding. Then he launched into his news. "I saw the stranger I think you're looking for! I was headed to your house to tell you, when I saw you turn the corner. I knew you'd want to know as soon as possible."

"Where did you see him?"

"In the park. You know that big old fallen-down shed they use to store equipment? We saw him come out of there. Quasi's following him now and so I came to get you."

"Did you tell the police?" Gracie asked, reaching for her cell phone to dial Rocky.

He shook his head. "The guy left, so we figured they wouldn't believe us anyway."

Rocky answered, and she updated him. They, too, decided to wait to call the police, since the man was still missing. Rocky first would call Stone and then meet her at the park. Gracie followed Chuckie, keeping to the perimeter where evergreens, shrubs and flowers created a hedge. She could see Pastor Paul's house. It made her shudder to think how easily it could be watched.

Martin jumped from his hiding place in a large clump of lilac bushes. "Hey, Mrs. Parks!" He held up a hand for the high five.

"You about scared me to death!" She'd seen the kids do the greeting for which he was waiting, so she slapped his palm. "How are you, Martin?"

"Didn't mean to scare you! I love this private eye stuff." He grinned. "It might even be a career possibility."

Chuckie elbowed him. "You'll probably be the one they're investigating!"

"Hey, look who's talking!" He shoved his friend back.

"Anyway, Mrs. Parks," Martin began again in all serious-ness, "we got the idea of looking for this guy yesterday. We thought he might come back to the scene of his first crime.

Chuckie figures he's looking for something he didn't find, or he wouldn't have gone after the pastor—then you."

He glanced at his friend for confirmation. "We've been taking turns watching the pastor's house—playing it real incognito. We wander by his house, hang out here a bit shooting the breeze, then move on."

"We're hoping to catch the prowler everybody thinks is me." Chuckie's tone was wry.

Martin laughed. But his loyalty to his friend was obvious now. Gracie decided their fashion statement had caused each of them similar problems. For dressing as they did, they all had probably been judged unfairly at one time or another.

"Did you know, Mrs. Parks," Martin told her, lightening the mood, "Old Lady McCall talks to those flowers?" He pointed to the marigold edging. "She plucks the tops off, saying, 'there you go, now you'll feel better.' I've even heard her tell them when to expect rain."

Gracie chuckled, imagining Louise doing that, but shook her finger in playful reprimand. "She's a lovely woman. She deserves more respect than being called Old Lady McCall."

"It's not like I would call her that to her face." Martin was obviously embarrassed. "She's okay—a little weird, but a nice old lady." Looking at Gracie, he added. "And, of course, a lot, lot older than you."

That made her laugh. "Weirdness is subjective, Martin. I'm

thinking that is something you boys and Mrs. McCall have in common."

They laughed with her. "Maybe eccentricity is a better word," Chuckie offered.

"And we Willow Benders can be quirky, there's no doubt," Gracie said, including herself. But she needed to be serious. "Chuckie, you could have gotten yourselves in trouble watching Pastor Meyer's house. You know you are still suspect."

Gracie could almost see the chip on his shoulder reappear, and regretted her warning. Silently she lifted his bruised soul to heaven. She didn't know Chuckie's family well or his circumstances, but she intuited he was in need of healing, the kind of healing only God could provide.

Chuckie kept his focus on the ground. "I had to do something. I feel real bad about the pastor. It's true, I hated him because he called the police on us but. . . ." He watched her through downturned eyes. "We did give him a hard time. He was trying to be cool, inviting us to youth group and all—"

"We even took him up on it," Martin interjected. "But some kids think we're losers—misfits. If you're not like everybody else, you don't fit in anywhere."

Church should be the place everybody fits, Gracie wanted to tell the boys. There were no misfits in the kingdom of God, and no one was ever excluded. She wanted to address these things, but knew this was not the time. Instead she said,

"People can be cruel. Different sometimes scares us. The best we can do is give others another chance."

"Seventy times seven chances." Chuckie was looking at her. He remembered. "Yes," she said, her heart full of love for this boy. "We forgive seventy times seven, if that's what it takes."

"Man, I'd lose track trying to forgive that many times."

She smiled. "That's the point. That's the way God is."

Chuckie scuffed the toe of his sneaker in the grass. "I felt bad about what happened to Pastor Meyer. And I hate the idea of you not feeling safe, Mrs. Parks."

She patted his back, sensing he did not want her to show the emotion she was feeling. "Thank you for caring, Chuckie."

"It's not like the police are going to do anything," Martin told her. "Not that they can do much, considering the circumstances. It seems as if that guy can make himself practically invisible."

She nodded. "We could call this the Case of the Invisible Stranger." Gracie crossed her arms and gave the boys her attention. "So, now tell me, what's been going on? Start from the beginning."

"Like I said," Chuckie told her, "we've been taking turns watching, but not all the time. We don't want to draw attention to ourselves. Sometimes we drive by, other times, we walk. It was Quasi who thought of sitting in those bushes. He used to come here to smoke."

Chuckie pointed to the house overlooking the park. "His grandmother lives there, and he used to stay with her while his parents worked."

"We only set up surveillance here this morning," Martin said in his best professional tone. "Wish we would have thought of it earlier. We might have had this case sewn up days ago!"

Martin waved her to follow him to the shed and the dirty, wire-mesh window on the back side. She peered in as he pointed out the spot where the man must have slept. There were many cigarette butts ground into the cement floor. It looked like he'd used a drop-cloth for a blanket.

"Not much of a lock." Martin pointed to the door. "Before you came I picked it—easy as pie!"

Gracie resisted the urge to lecture him about that.

"We should move," Chuckie told them. "He might come back."

"Good point!" Martin looked at Gracie, eyes bright. "You can hide in the bushes with us."

Suddenly she saw Rocky was approaching with Bruce Stone and breathed a sigh of relief. She wouldn't have to crawl through branches and brush to appease the boy detectives. "Thanks, guys, but here come my friends. We'll just take a stroll through the park, and no one will be the wiser as I update them."

Gracie introduced everyone, and then Martin spilled the

whole story before she had time to suggest the walk. Quasi came running up to them, practically bulldozing Chuckie.

"I lost him." Quasi burst out. "I think the guy figured out that I was following him. He ducked down the alley over there—real deliberate. I tried to follow him, but he cut through somebody's yard. I couldn't tell which—about every dog in Willow Bend was barking."

He looked at Gracie. "I'm sorry, Mrs. Parks, we really wanted to get him!"

"We'll wait him out," Martin declared.

Rocky shook his head, putting a hand on Martin's shoulder. "I think we'll leave it to Mr. Stone and the police. He's with the Immigration service and wants to arrest and deport the man."

He looked at Quasi. "It's important you stay out of this, especially if he's seen you. We don't know if this guy is dangerous."

"I don't think he is," Stone said, "but we shouldn't take any chances. I'll call Chief Bower." He looked at the teenagers. "We'll take it from here, boys."

Chuckie snorted. "They won't do anything. They could have put out an APB, roadblocks—the works. They could have searched the town! Instead, they went after a bunch of kids just because we dress weird, and hang out in the park!"

Gracie narrowed her gaze. "You're not being fair, Chuckie. To the best of their ability, Herb and his men have been on the job. You said it yourself, the man has made himself practically invisible. He's managed to stay unseen for almost a week."

"We can't just let him get away, not when we're this close!" Chuckie punched his palm with his other fist. "I wish I would have jumped the guy when I had the chance."

Gracie wanted to warn him about his temper, but she simply said that she appreciated his concern and all that they'd done to help. He seemed to relax, admitting they, too, had lost the guy and that he wasn't likely to return to the park.

"I can reach you on your cell phone, right?" Stone was looking at Rocky. He answered in the affirmative, and Stone turned to Quasi. "Suppose you show me right where you lost the guy. We'll wait out on the sidewalk for the police, then go in my car."

Stone phoned Herb, but got Jim, who said he'd be there directly. Gracie wondered how they'd work together, then decided what would happen was out of her hands, anyway.

"I'll buy you a cup of coffee," Rocky suggested. "I could go for another one of Abe's breakfast specials."

Her laughter helped her to relax. She had put the whole situation in God's hands already, so there was no use fussing. She looked fondly at Rocky. "You and El were always taking care of your stomachs. Top priority."

"Some cultures say it is the stomach, not the heart, that is the center of emotion, Gracie. I think they just might be right. Besides, it's what an army travels upon!"

Abe was just taking fresh cherry strudel out of the oven. The ceiling fan swirled, blending cinnamon and warm yeast with a faint hint of mint. Mother Wasserman's chicken soup!

"Hello, lovely lady," Abe called from the kitchen. And peeking through the short-order window, he said to Rocky, "One breakfast special coming up!"

He returned, wiping his hands on his apron. "The special is still two ninety-five and—"

"Advice is free," Rocky finished.

"I might have raised the price." Abe chuckled. "I'm getting popular, you know. A sage, Gracie called me."

"Don't let it go to your head!" she warned him playfully.

He changed directions, setting three cups on the counter. "Has that guy shown up again, the one who was in here, that you wanted to know about?" He filled them, then slid one to Gracie and another to Rocky. Abe spooned several heaping teaspoons of sugar into his, which never failed to take Gracie aback. "Abe," she liked to protest. "Don't you think you're sweet enough as you are?"

Rocky drank his coffee black. "We've got a lead, but he's gone to ground. Seems invisible. Maybe he's left town. . . ."

"No, I don't think so," Abe surprised them by saying. "Everyone who's eaten here returns, even the best caterer in town." He winked at Gracie.

Rocky's jaw dropped. "You mean he's been back? And you didn't call?"

"You didn't ask me to."

Rocky threw up his hands. "I didn't ask! I didn't *ask*, he says! Why do you think I was questioning you about him in the first place?"

"How do *I* know why you ask questions? You're the newspaperman. Reporters always ask questions. A snoopy bunch." He turned to go the kitchen, but paused. "Besides, you think I read minds? I can tell what you think? Not even a sage can do that." Abe called over his shoulder going into the kitchen, "You still want that special?"

Rocky growled, but said yes. "So when was he here?"

"Yesterday, late afternoon. Had the afternoon special—turkey club and coleslaw."

"Did you talk to him?" Gracie wanted to know. "Did you mention we were looking for him?"

Abe turned around and threw hands up this time. "I didn't know you were looking for him, remember? I asked him if he found a church though. Eternal Hope. Said he had family who went there—a niece."

"He said that?" Gracie looked at Rocky.

Abe nodded. "Maria, the little girl the pastor's parents adopted. He said he went to visit her, but the neighbor told him that she was staying with you. So I gave him your address—thought you had choir practice, though."

She couldn't believe it. The audacity of the man! Vincente Juarez was not only *very* visible, but was out in the open with his intentions. He must have gone to the church, seen her leave her keys in the car, and seized the opportunity to take them. He probably knew she'd be there a couple of hours at least.

What about Uncle Miltie? He had been in the house. That meant Juarez had taken a great risk—for what? He couldn't have known the old man was up before sunrise and that he often went to bed just after the sun set. The poor dear would often spend the wee hours walking the floor with indigestion. A fact that wasn't helped by his unwillingness to take anything for it!

Juarez must have waited for the old man to go to bed. It made her shudder to think of him looking in her front windows. He must have bided his time until Uncle Miltie went upstairs, then simply unlocked the door and walked into her house.

What was he looking for?

"You okay, Gracie?" Rocky's grasp on her arm was firm. "You went pale on us. Are you feeling all right?"

She nodded, embarrassed that she'd let fear so get the better of her. "I just can't believe he was that brazen—unlocking my door and walking right in!"

Abe was standing over her now. "Who is this man really?"

"He's after something," Rocky said. "He's been in Gracie's house looking for something. He attacked Paul Meyer to get it."

Abe thumped his forehead with the palm of his hand. "And I helped him. Stupid, stupid, stupid."

221

"You didn't know," Gracie told him.

He shook his head. "I should have known—the man had bad eyes."

As they unfolded the developments of the preceding week, Abe kept shaking his head. Gracie then updated Rocky on her conversation with Maria and Harold. The mysterious man was in fact Maria's uncle, but what did he want and what was he looking for?

When Gracie pulled into her driveway, she saw John Griswold on the sidewalk in front of her house. He had Samson on a leash. The dog was unusually sedate. John looked like he wanted to talk, so she waved and walked over to meet him.

"The mutt is hyperactive," John told her, apparently realizing that she was studying the terrier. "The vet gave him medication—something like Prozac for dogs, I guess. He's been a pussycat ever since. We were worried he'd attack someone else."

Gracie braved stroking Samson's ears.

"He's got an obsession for hedges, though. Digging and rutting around in Hadlock's, and now yours. I'm real sorry about that." John met her gaze and pointed toward the hydrangeas on the side of the house. "I fixed the wood-chip mulch covering as best I could. Hope it is all right."

Gracie walked to her bushes where the mulch had been redistributed. She bent to look for what the dog may have been rooting. There at base of her bushes were cigarette butts—a half dozen of them ground into the dirt, rubbed into the ground with the same ferocity she'd seen earlier that day.

"He didn't do any real damage, did he?" John was saying. "I caught him in the act. He's like a canine natural disaster simulator! Told the vet that when I took him in for boosters."

She told John it was fine. Perhaps she seemed a bit too eager to get rid of him, because he looked genuinely hurt. She excused herself, explaining she had a lot to do.

Gracie immediately walked around the side of her house, through her backyard, and across the alley to the Hadlocks' hedges. It wasn't hard to follow Samson's trail of destruction to another pile of cigarette butts.

Juarez *had* been there the night Maria played in the yard.

15

LATER THAT DAY, Gracie dropped in on Marge in hopes that browsing for a gift for Wendy's new dance studio would take her mind off the elusive Juarez. Marge was finishing up with a customer, so Gracie scanned the shelves. Her friend's shop did have an eclectic selection. There were shell necklaces and gourd bowls and patchwork scarves and chenille tea cozies. It reflected Marge's personality in ways both easy and hard to see.

For one thing, Marge prided herself on her fashion sense and fad savvy. She knew which and how many trendy trinkets would sell. But her true taste was more flamboyant. She had kept in stock the rainbow feather boas that had been dangling behind the counter for as long as Gracie could remember. She also offered gaudy earrings in the form of almost every animal and bird on the planet.

An oriental print sarong caught Gracie's eye. Sheer silk,

the wrap gave off a shimmering elegance. It would look lovely over her daughter-in-law's practice leotard. Wendy was slim and stylish, perfect for the sarong. It really wasn't something for the studio itself, however, and Gracie had her heart set on a gift that would show her support. She was pleased for Wendy, and proud of her son for backing her.

"I love it!" Marge said, coming up beside her. "But it isn't you. I can't imagine you in anything but comfortable. Lord, knows I've been trying to juice up your wardrobe for years."

Gracie put the garment back on the rack. "I was thinking of Wendy. She's gone back to dancing. Did I mention that?"

"You said she was thinking of it. I guess she decided then—and Arlen is fine with it?"

Gracie nodded, but her thoughts were elsewhere. She couldn't get the picture of Juarez hiding in the Hadlocks' bushes out of her head. It was going to be harder than she thought to keep her mind at ease, her heart untroubled. For that, she would need a miracle. She glanced in the usual direction, a quick prayer on her lips.

"So they're still the happy honeymooners. All is well in the Parks family?"

She smiled at her friend, sensing that was a loaded question. "They love each other, and for now that will carry them through. For the rest, they'll be leaning on the Lord."

"And you, Gracie dear, are you leaning on the Lord?" Marge held her gaze, anticipating that Gracie would pour out what was churning inside of her. Gracie was not so sure she was ready to face that. Undamming the geyser would not be pretty.

Without saying anything more, Marge took the sarong off the rack again. "I'll give you a good price on this."

She appreciated her friend's sensitivity. "Wendy would love it," Gracie conceded. "But I was thinking more of a studio warming gift."

"She *is* the studio." Marge winked. "And this would be a present for both of them, you know what I mean?

Gracie let herself laugh, trying to rein in her emotions. After all there was nothing she could do but wait: wait for Paul to heal, wait for Juarez to be found. "Patience was never a lesson I liked learning."

"Hmm?" Marge was looking at her. "What does patience have to do with buying this for your daughter-in-law?"

Gracie laughed again, realizing how strange it sounded to admit. "I was talking to God. I suppose you think it's odd."

"Not for you, dear. I sense your insides are all in knots over this mystery man who is wreaking havoc in our lives."

"He's not a mystery man anymore," Gracie opened up to her friend, telling her about their conversation with Abe, the experience with the boys, the cigarette butts and the Samson connection.

Marge hugged her. "You need a good stiff . . . knitting needle!"

"Knitting needle?"

"It's amazing how relaxing that can be. It takes enough concentration that you can't obsess and is mindless enough to give your brain a rest. You're coming to my house for dinner, and I'm calling the Layettes for Honduras gang to come over afterwards. We're going to click-click ourselves silly. And you, Gracie Parks, are going to laugh until your heart is rested."

Gracie liked the idea. "But what about Uncle Miltie?"

"Can he knit?" Marge chuckled. "Have him come over for dinner, too. I've got enough freezer fare for the three of us. He can mosey home whenever he's ready, or watch television at my place. He might like socializing with the group."

Served with Marge's flare for festivity, hot crusty bread and a tossed salad, prepackaged frozen lasagna became restaurant quality. She'd used her best china, linen napkins and candles, and put out a bouquet of red roses from her garden. Of course, Gracie couldn't go empty-handed, and so made a banana split dessert with lots of whipped cream and maraschino cherries. Uncle Miltie was in a frenzy of anticipation until it was served, then subsided in bliss.

"Everyone is coming at seven," Marge told Gracie as they finished the dishes. "I thought we'd have light refreshments." She opened a cupboard door to retrieve her stash of tea boxes. "I have some cookies—and your leftover dessert."

She glanced Gracie's way. "You think we need coffee?"

"No, tea's enough. If anyone wants coffee, you have instant, don't you?"

"Nothing but!"

She stacked her collection on the counter. "Ginger Spice, Peppermint Dreams, Chamomile Night—ah, and my favorite, Tangerine Tango." Marge was not only a connoisseur of freezer fare, but she had a fancy for exotic teas, as well.

"I think tea and cookies will be perfect," Gracie told her.

Uncle Miltie folded the newspaper. "That's that! There's not much in the news. I suppose that's the best. We've got a safe little town here—an oasis of sorts."

Gracie couldn't help but wonder if that hadn't changed. At that moment, Willow Bend did not seem such a safe place to her.

"You girls enjoy yourselves. I have an appointment with Andy Griffith tonight." Miltie got himself out his chair slowly with the help of his cane.

It pleased Gracie that he didn't have to rely on the walker so much anymore. She sensed that he was proud of himself, too. Yet it sapped his energy, that was also apparent. To save his strength, she would have to insist that he rely more on his walker around the house. "I'll be home by nine," she assured him.

"No hurry, dear." He paused at the threshold. "I'm going to take that stomach relaxant again. Slept like a baby the other night." His expression turned serious. "That was probably the one night I should have played the martyr, as you call it." He shook his head, pondering a moment. "I never conked out like that before."

"Well, that explains why you didn't hear the prowler." Marge's tone was edgy. "You should have mentioned that."

Miltie nodded. "Didn't give it much thought at the time."

Marge turned to Gracie. "Now, we are *not*, do you hear me, *not* going to obsess on this. I know what you are thinking! You think that crazy Juarez, whoever and wherever he is, slipped Miltie a Mickey Finn. But you can't know that for sure, Gracie, so don't speculate. You're going to make yourself sick over this case."

"Uncle Miltie did have milk," Gracie defended. "I remember putting the glass in the dishwasher."

Marge wagged her finger. "We're not discussing it! You're going to have fun tonight! Fun, fun, fun! Then you're going to get a good night's sleep—even if I have to slip *you* a Mickey Finn." Her eyes flashed mischief. "You can resume your sleuthing obsession with Inspector Gravino in the morning."

Gracie threw up her hands in defeat. There was no point in arguing with Marge. The woman could always play her ultimate trump card, and tease her about Rocky. And there was no convincing her friend there could be nothing between the man and herself. She and Rocky were just friends.

A light breakfast seemed in order. Gracie fixed cinnamon toast to go with the sliced melon. She pretended not to see Uncle Miltie fumble making coffee, smiling inside at the boyishness that had endured in him for eight decades. He *was* trying to be helpful. She sensed he, too, was concerned about her well-being. This morning she felt terrific.

It was going to be a glorious day. Marge had been right, knitting had been just what she'd needed to get her mind off her troubles. She had to admit that she'd slept better than she had in days.

Rick had made her laugh the night before, sparring gently with Estelle. He countered her grousing with good-natured ribbing. It was all a matter of attitude, Gracie decided; a person could be grumbly hateful, or gratefully humble. Rick was a prime example of the latter.

This morning's prayer walk would feature praise songs. She had a lot to be thankful for—especially good friends, as always!

The phone rang as Gracie returned from her walk. She was thrilled to her Jean Meyer joyfully announcing to her that Paul was back with them. And there seemed to be no lasting complications, although his memory was still sketchy. Dr. Wright was on his way to the hospital and Jean wanted to be there, too, so she was hoping Gracie could come right over because Maria was still asleep.

"Of course!" Gracie exclaimed, her heart practically bursting with excitement. "I'll change my clothes and be right there."

She hung up, noticing a note from Uncle Miltie that he had left for the senior center. She scribbled one to him, leaving the Meyers' telephone number. Jean was waiting and ready when she arrived. She hugged her friend, who bubbled with additions to her glad tidings. Paul had eaten a little breakfast, and complained about it being practically all liquid. Amazingly, there was a good possibility of his coming home the next day, where he would heal more quickly in his own surroundings. Gracie decided not to ask if he had identified his attacker. They would know soon enough.

Maria came down about an hour later and, after greeting Gracie, headed right to the cupboard. "Would you like to have some cereal with me?"

"How about we make Monster Toast?"

A perplexed smile.

Gracie mixed several small dishes of assorted food colorings with milk and gave Maria a paintbrush to paint faces on bread. Doña Coca sat on the table to watch them toast monster faces and sprinkle them with cinnamon sugar. Gracie told the child the wonderful news. They chatted about Paul's homecoming, then Maria asked about Suzy and expressed apprehension about her first day of school, which was upcoming.

"We'll get you girls together more, now that your brother is coming home," Gracie told her. "Suzy will tell you everything you need to know. I'll talk to your mother about getting you taken on a tour. Perhaps Suzy and I could join you."

Maria grinned. "I would like that." She looked at the doll. "Doña says this is the most wonderful day!"

"That it is!" Gracie hugged her. "Let's make time right now to tell God how much we appreciate him."

Maria reached for the doll and they each held one of Doña Coca's hands. Gracie began, and the child finished, "for all your blessings we are grateful, señor. But for me it is for the family you give, and especially the health of my new brother. She slipped easily into her native tongue, *"Oramos en el nombre de nuestro Señor Jesucristo. Amén."*

Gracie was touched, guessing it to be a similar closing: we pray in the name our our Lord Jesus Christ. Amen.

Uncle Miltie arrived at the Meyers' in time for lunch and, after devouring a sandwich, decided to work on the new front door lying across sawhorses on the back porch. "Paul's been talking about finishing it for weeks. I'll get it painted and call Roy to help me install it. A nice homecoming surprise, don't you think?"

"That's a great idea!" Plans for a party came to mind. As soon as Gracie heard from Jean, she'd get the ball rolling. But, for the moment, she would concentrate on ingredients for soup. Checking the freezer for vegetables, she discovered frozen bread dough. Nothing like the aroma of fresh bread to warm the soul. It would be her surprise!

Maria kept Uncle Miltie company as Gracie worked in the kitchen. It was late afternoon before Jean came home.

"It smells delicious!"

At the sound of her mother's voice, Maria bounded into

the kitchen. She threw her arms around her mother. "When is my brother coming home?"

"Tomorrow!" Jean beamed. "The doctor says there is no need to keep him. He's doing just fine. He'll have to go back to be checked, of course. But he's coming home tomorrow!"

Gracie couldn't keep her arms down. "Praise the Lord!"

"God is good," Jean exclaimed.

"All the time!" She finished. "God is good."

Maria clapped her hands, giggling. "We must have a party! I will make a big sign. There is paper in my brother's study."

They watched Maria scurry about, collecting magic markers, scissors and stickers. Gracie hated to broach the inevitable. "Did he identify his attacker?"

"No." Jean glanced at Maria. "He seems to have lost that day practically altogether. We reminded him of what we knew, but a lot of things are still hazy in his mind. He was having problems with aligning many of his short-term memories on a timeline. The doctor says that's to be expected. We'll wait. For now we'll just be thankful he's back with us."

Later, when the knock came, Gracie was sure it was probably Rocky since she had left a message telling him she would be staying with Jean, so she got the door. In front of her stood a dark-skinned man wearing sunglasses. Vincente!

Her heart raced. Gracie gripped the doorknob tighter in order to help maintain her sangfroid.

"Good day, señora."

She wanted to slam the door, to push him away! But he stood there patiently, as if expecting her to invite him into the house. Could he not know they knew? *Oh, dear Lord!*

"Who is at the door?" Jean said, coming up behind her.

Vincente humbled his gaze a moment. "Señora Meyer, finally we meet. I am Vincente Juarez, the uncle of Maria Juarez Vidal. I am in your country a short time—only a day." He glanced between them, the sunglasses protecting his intentions from being seen. "I mean no harm. I simply want to visit my niece. I am flying out of Chicago tomorrow."

Jean stepped to the door. "How did you know where to find us?

"May I come in?" He took off his glasses. "I will explain."

Gracie did not want to tip their hand, but she didn't want the man to come inside, either. She eyed Jean, wondering if the woman was thinking the same.

It was Maria who made their decision. "Tío Vincente!" She darted between the women and hugged the man, rattling rapid Spanish. Before Gracie had time to react, Maria ushered her uncle into the living room to sit down.

Jean shot Gracie a panicked look, she could only shrug in return. Then it came to her! "Mr. Juarez, would you like refreshment?"

"No, no, that is not necess—"

"Yes, we would," Maria cut in. "I will get them."

Jean interceded. "No dear, you stay with your uncle. Mrs. Parks and I will get them."

In the kitchen Jean grabbed Gracie's shoulders. "What are we going to do?"

Gracie pulled out her cell phone. "You fix the iced tea. I'll call Stone, the INS guy."

He said he'd be there in minutes with police backup. "Don't scare the man," Gracie warned him. "We don't know if he's dangerous."

"We'll be careful, trust me, Mrs. Parks."

She wanted to, desperately.

Uncle Miltie came in the back door. "In time for refreshments. I'll let that second coat dry, and maybe tonight Roy and I can get it hung." He recognized, suddenly, that a problem had arisen. "What's wrong?

Gracie lowered her voice and explained, suggesting Uncle Miltie introduce himself. As hosts, they would personify graciousness until help arrived. She decided to call Rocky, too, for good measure. Jean continued filling the glasses, while Uncle Miltie ambled to the next room.

Gracie was just hanging up when Maria dashed by to grab the doll from the kitchen counter. "Tío Vincente wants to see her."

The doll! That must be what the man wanted. Gracie hurried to rejoin the group.

Uncle Miltie was already in the middle of a joke. "So, why

don't you see any dead crows on the road, huh? There's always one on the wire calling, caw, caw, caw."

The visitor's chuckle seemed strained.

Gracie took her place on the chair beside the couch where Maria had seated herself, hugging the doll. Her uncle sat beside her. Gracie prayed silently for their safety, for calmness and, above all else, love for this man she wanted to hate.

"Here we are, iced tea and Gracie's famous peanut butter bars." Jean said in an unbelievably cheery tone, setting a tray on the coffee table. "Do you like peanut butter, Señor Juarez?" She handed him a glass. "We've discovered it's uniquely North American. Most Europeans we meet either haven't had it or don't like it."

She looked at Gracie, who was still amazed by Jean's composure. "Maria ate peanut butter for the first time while she was with us. But she likes it, right, dear?" A smile to her daughter.

"And you, Señor?" She handed him a bar on a napkin.

He took a bite. "Very good, thank you."

A gracious smile. Jean sat down across from the man. "And why did you say you are in the United States?"

"Business—in Chicago." A nervous twitch passed across his face. "I represent a company negotiating with American investors. As I have said, I am in the States but a few days. I had meetings until today."

He turned toward Maria. "Today I make time for my lovely niece. May I see La Doña?" She handed the doll to him, and Vincente said to Jean, "She told you that my beloved mother made this for her. My mother was very talented. A saint, God rest her soul. Maria is fortunate to have a memento."

"Indeed." Jean kept her gaze on the man. "Now, that we have become acquainted, you will have to give us your address and phone number. We will be returning to Tegucigalpa in January."

His smile was gracious. "I am between addresses right now, as you can appreciate. But I will see that you get it. You are still with the same Christian agency?" He paused, then said, "Perhaps Señoras—Señor, I could have a little time alone with Maria . . . to remember, to say good-bye."

Jean's "Certainly!" surprised Gracie.

Uncle Miltie was the first to stand, excusing himself to clean up his paint mess. "It was a pleasure meeting you, Mr. Juarez."

Jean stood. "If you'll excuse me, I have some watering to do. The planters on the front porch."

Gracie was at a loss. What was the plan?

The key turned in the front door lock. Harold Meyer walked in, followed by his son.

"Paul!" Jean exclaimed as the door swung open.

Vincente Juarez jumped up. A whirl of confusion ensued, until Maria cried, "Doña Coca!" And the next thing Gracie knew Vincente lay flat, with on his face pressed against the floor, pinned there by Uncle Miltie who was leaning on his walker, the very walker he had used to trip him. "Help me here, Harold. Gracie, you get some rope!"

THE WHOLE SCENE HAD UNFOLDED in a matter of seconds, but to Gracie, it felt like an eternity. They were sitting in the pastor's living room, having iced tea. Across from her was a man tied to a kitchen chair, and he, too, was attempting to figure out exactly what had happened.

When Paul entered the house, their guest apparently had panicked. Uncle Miltie, bless his heart, had had the where-withal to trip the man when he tried to escape with Maria's doll. Gracie glanced at her uncle, who was practically bursting at the seams with pride at the part he'd played in the apprehension of their number-one suspect.

Herb Bower and Bruce Stone had just arrived with Rocky on their heels. They joined in singing Uncle Miltie's praises. There would be no living with her uncle!

Paul told them he had recognized Vincente Juarez right away. His memory, it seemed, was much better than they first had thought. Earlier, after being examined, the doctor had been agreeable to discharging him the following morning. It had been Paul who'd wanted to leave that day, promising rest under the watchful care of his parents. They'd decided to surprise his mother.

As he detailed for them now the events leading up to the attack, Vincente simply stared, jaw set and shoulders straight.

Paul told them Juarez had seemed to appear out of nowhere. "I was in the sanctuary waiting for Lester, and noticed when I turned the lights on that a couple of bulbs were out. I decided to change them, since I couldn't get into my office because I'd forgotten my keys."

"But the front door was open." Gracie reminded him.

"The sexton had opened it. Luckily, he was just finishing what he was doing. Opening the front door seemed the least bother, and I was going to meet Lester in the sanctuary, anyway."

It was Jean who asked, "So where are your keys, honey? They're not on the rack in the kitchen."

"I don't know."

"When did you have them last?"

"I'm not sure," he said sheepishly. "I forget them often, and Pat is usually there before me, so I usually buzz her to let me in. I could have misplaced them weeks ago, I guess."

Herb cleared his throat. "Let's discuss the keys later, tell us what happened next."

Paul told them that he'd just gotten off the ladder when Juarez appeared out of nowhere. He greeted the man, who said he was out walking and saw the church door ajar. Vincente had told him he just wanted to pray, and chosen a seat in a pew, while Paul went back to changing the bulbs. It was then that Paul had heard Pat, and excused himself to talk to her. "That's the last thing I remember."

Paul studied Vincente Juarez seemingly without the slightest acrimony. "I had the ladder: I was going to put it back. I remember your face . . . scared. It's only a feeling—I don't remember what happened next."

"He must have hit you with something that bruised your temple and sent you tumbling backward," Gracie said, trying to make sense out of everything. She looked at Juarez. "You stood the ladder back up. Why?"

No response.

"The doll!" Paul exclaimed. "She sat on the pew. The ladder would have fallen across it. He moved it to get the doll. By that time, Pat was coming. She was talking to Maria, who had gone to the bathroom. She left the doll on the front pew. She'd been playing the piano for me."

"So Pat was in the the front vestibule." Gracie remembered the church secretary saying that she heard voices. "Harold came in the back entrance, so you were trapped," she said to Vincente.

"You slipped out during the confusion, but you couldn't get the doll because you didn't have time. By then, Harold had found his son."

Gracie knew she was right, and sensed Maria's uncle squirm. "You slipped into that side foyer, which explains why that door was ajar. No one ever uses that door because it sticks, so it never closes properly. That side entrance is often not even noticed, it's practically hidden by the stairway to the choir loft."

Paul sat down beside his attacker. The pastor's expression was kind. "For the sake of your niece," he began softly, "tell us the truth. I don't think you meant to hurt me. I think you really moved the ladder to see how badly I was hurt. I want to believe that if God had not brought my father that moment, you would have helped me."

Maria started to cry, and Jean put her arm around the child. It almost broke Gracie's heart to watch. Maria stepped away, struggling to regain control. She brushed away tears and walked to face her uncle. Her bottom lip trembled, as she spoke to her uncle in Spanish. Gracie had the feeling the Honduran was getting a familiar earful, probably similar to a lecture Maria had once heard her mother or grandmother give.

He broke down and tears came to his eyes. His response in Spanish was tender, so obviously moving that Maria hugged him tight, and then sat in his lap.

"She told him that her grandmother always believed in

him," Rocky said, interpreting the scene they'd just witnessed. "His father would say Vincente was no good, but his mother knew better. She said this son only wanted his father's respect. The things he did were wrong, but he did them to try to earn his father's love."

Rocky was obviously struggling with emotion, too. He paused a moment and Maria finished, "He must make this right. He must confess and ask for mercy. He must not dishonor my grandmother in this way. She loved him. I heard her say it many times."

She looked at her uncle. "I told him that *Abuelito* said he loved him. I heard him tell my mother that was the reason he disowned him. It broke his heart, but he felt it was the only way. We are an honorable family."

Her uncle nodded. "I know I must make it right for the sake of my parents. And my beautiful niece, my only family."

Gracie wiped her tears and she noticed the others seemed as affected by the scene. "We want to help you, for Maria's sake."

"I am not worthy."

Maria bubbled. "But Jesus is! El Señor has already forgiven you. He loves you and gave these people to show the way back to Him. You only need to look. He is here."

It was as if the message she gave them held each one in a warm embrace. Juarez did not say anything for a long time, but Gracie sensed God working in his heart.

"It is as you say, Pastor," he began. "I only wanted to get by you. I shoved you hard, you stumbled with that ladder and I pushed again, hoping you would fall backwards and I would have enough time to escape. You fell, but I did not anticipate the baptismal, which you would strike. I saw the blood and wanted to help. I put the doll back. You see, she was in my hands, I could have run away. But I knew what I must do. I moved the ladder to help you."

Stone finally addressed Vincente in Spanish. The man nodded, his expression penitent.

"He's got assault and battery to answer to, at the very least," Herb reminded them.

"He is not a U.S. citizen," Stone reminded him. "Technically, he has a valid visa, so I can't arrest him unless you press charges. I will take him into custody, though. I have some questions we want to ask him. He will be deported and the charges will follow him to Honduras."

"What I want to know is, why?" Rocky was in his face. "You nearly killed a man. Stalked others, invaded their privacy—for what? What is in the doll?"

Maria hopped off her uncle's lap, and ran to retrieve Doña Coca. She handed her to Jean. "Be gentle."

Jean turned to Stone. "Can we untie him? I think he should do this. He should turn over whatever is in the doll."

Juarez took the doll gently. He lifted the skirt to reveal the bandaged belly. "I do not want to do this in front of the child."

"I've got a ripper in my sewing box," Jean told him. "Let's you and I take Doña Coca and get it."

Rocky glared at Maria's uncle. "Don't even think about trying anything."

"I could go with you," Herb said.

Jean smiled. "I don't think it's necessary. Señor Juarez and I will do a little operation and be back."

"Doña Jean, it is okay!" Maria said. "Open her here. I want to hold her hand. I want to be one to repair the tear."

Jean brought the ripper and Maria laid the doll on the table, holding a hand. Everyone gathered around. Juarez snipped the threads ever so tenderly. Harold stepped behind Maria, encircling her in an embrace.

White cotton batting. Gasps. Gracie thought of the book she had read so many times to Arlen. *The Velveteen Rabbit* had been loved into reality. Doña Coca, however, had been forced into reality under far different circumstances.

Maria's uncle probed deep into the cavity to retrieve three small cut stones. Shining ones, reflecting the light.

Diamonds.

More gasps.

It was Rocky who reached to take them. "Well, I'll be!"

"Are they real?" Herb asked.

Juarez nodded.

Miltie was at his shoulder. "You've got a scoop!"

Rocky just grinned.

Gracie smiled, too. God had worked a miracle in that room, and for this day, it was the only scoop worth noting.

The diamonds had been an extortion payment to Carlos Martinez, the politician for whom Maria's mother had worked. It turned out that Vincente had overheard a discussion between Martinez and the man who had paid him to pass off a fake historical land grant. When the maneuver was discovered and Carlos implicated, Vincente knew what was really going on, because Cleo, his sister, had overheard a conversation between Martinez and his wife, as they talked about cashing in the gems used as payment.

Maria's uncle had the idea of snatching the jewels, but the police arrived to arrest Martinez before he could escape with them. He sewed them into the tummy of Maria's doll, hoping to recover them at a later date. In the meantime, the hurricane had hit—and his sister had been killed in the mudslide that claimed their village. He assumed Maria had been with her mother.

Several months later, however, Juarez spotted Maria's photograph in a newspaper feature on the relief effort, and discovered she'd been adopted by American missionaries planning to return to the United States. The story had also mentioned Paul and where his church was, so finding Maria had been easy.

"What I want to know," Rocky said, after listening to Juarez's confession, "is why the cosmetic bag? And did you take the pastor's keys?"

Vincente looked at Paul. "Yes, and no. I thought the jewelry might be real. The pearls looked real. I thought it would be less suspicious getting rid of the diamonds if it seemed I was pawning family jewelry."

He smiled. "For a man who handled diamonds valued in the hundreds of thousands of dollars, yes? I could not tell the genuine from the fake."

It was the same with most things, Gracie reasoned; the gaudy and the sacred were often confused. She looked at Maria standing next to her uncle who was still sitting at the table. She had her arms locked around his shoulders. His hand was on hers.

"Love is the Diamond, isn't it, Lord?" She closed her eyes, seeking God's presence. He was teaching them something, she could feel it. "But its value is not measured in dollars."

When she looked up, all eyes were on her. "I couldn't help thinking that Vincente's plans were confounded each step of the way. He couldn't get away with the diamonds, the doll got away from him, and Love caught him in the end."

Rocky nodded, and she wondered if he was pondering these things in *his* heart. "It does appear this is the crime that was not meant to be."

"Because God works all things for good," Maria told him. "He does that for those who love Him."

Barb Jennings made a grand entrance in an embroidered skirt and peasant blouse. She clapped her hands. "Choir, places!"

Excitement practically bubbled as the group of festively costumed singers trooped to the choir loft. Gracie took a moment to fix the bright woven shawl Jean had lent her.

"See you later, Señora Gracie," Rocky said softly as he came up beside her.

"Salsa seems as unexpected here as it would on a bagel," Abe quipped, giving Gracie a quick hug.

Gracie kissed Abe's cheek. "We can all use a little more spice in our lives." This time, she meant it even more emphatically.

"You go, girl!" Uncle Miltie exclaimed.

Gracie gently shook her maracas and her shoulders. "Wait until you hear the music. We're going to whip up a truly celestial salsa!" She gave another shake before scurrying after the rest of the choir.

She took her place beside Don Delano, who was wearing a red western-style shirt and a straw cowboy hat.

As Don slapped the beat on the kettle drum, Gracie got her arms going to the Latin tempo. Her spirits soared, and for twenty minutes she almost believed that rhythm from south-of-the-border flowed naturally through her very being. What an amazing event—so vibrant, so joyful, so contagious in its feeling of celebration. Even Estelle had gotten her groove!

Margie wore a stylish sarong. Her dozens of bracelets were clinking in sync to the music. *"Gracias á la vida,"* they sang.

Out in front of her, she could see only dear friends. It looked like half of Willow Bend had turned out to consecrate Layettes for Honduras. Gracie was indeed thankful!

The meal catered by Gracie and Jean was a big hit, too. And special recognition went to Maria and her tortilla crew.

"I've never seen anything quite like it," Estelle said, studying the white wicker bassinet trimmed with brilliant red, green and yellow rayon scarves.

"Irresistible," Tish Ball agreed. "Like just about everything in Marge's shop."

Estelle sat the doll she'd made on a heaping pile of packaged cloth diapers, pins, undershirts, and sleepers, surrounded by fifty pairs of booties.

"Muy bonita!" Maria held Doña Coca up to see her new friend.

Marge dabbed the corners of her eyes. "That's the sweetest touch, Estelle. A grandma doll to travel with the layettes. American grandmas and mamas to the babies of Honduras."

"Don't forget the papas." Rick came up beside her, holding a plate heaping with tortilla chips and salsa.

Marge wrapped her arm around his waist. "No, indeed."

"Hey, I fixed and painted the bassinet," Uncle Miltie reminded them. "Add grandpa to that list." He hugged Maria. "I'm the adoptable kind, right."

He winked at Maria. "Offer me a warm tortilla and I'll follow you anywhere."

Gracie felt radiant. *Gracias á la vida!*

It was later that they learned the the rest of the story. Over coffee, Abe read the news to Gracie from Rocky's paper. "It says here that INS Investigator Bruce Stone followed a trail of corruption implicating a prominent politician and a several American and Honduran expatriates.

"Vincente Juarez will testify, according to Stone."

"Stone," Rocky said. "A good man, even if he did wear sunglasses!"

Gracie smiled, remembering something Stone had told her. "For a man who thought he already had reached his level of incompetence, it certainly turned out to be quite the opposite," she said.

Abe put down the paper and topped their coffee cups.

"Only goes to show there is hope for all of us," Gracie told him. "Her uncle and Maria have been corresponding. The Meyers have been his advocates with the Honduran government. They are hoping to get diplomatic immunity for the man, perhaps put him to work with their ecumenical agency. Regardless, Maria says she will visit him on a regular basis when she returns with them to Honduras."

"Did you ever find out whether or not he'd somehow put

something in Miltie's drink?" Rocky asked. "I don't remember ever confirming that suspicion or not."

"He says he didn't. He just had stood in the Hadlocks' hedge and watched. Uncle Miltie's room is at the rear of the house. Vincente waited until my uncle pulled the blinds, then gave him fifteen minutes to fall asleep. He used my key to unlock the front door."

She sighed, feeling vulnerable once again. "Anyway, we figured it was probably the stomach relaxant. Wouldn't you know, the one drug he agrees to use makes him practically comatose!"

"Juarez told us he was only looking for the doll," Rocky continued. "He thought Maria was staying with Gracie. He checked the bedrooms, careful not to disturb anything."

Rocky glanced at her. "And he thought he had replaced the pillows correctly, but he didn't count on our super sleuth."

Gracie brushed that flattery away with the flick of her hand, and remembered her conversation with John Griswold. "Turns out the dog hates dark sunglasses!"

"Smart dog," Abe said.

"Sunglasses? How do you know?"

She explained that she'd taken Gooseberry for his rabies booster, and the vet had told her. The Griswolds, it seems, had decided to take Samson back to the shelter. There the assistant suddenly remembered the previous owner mentioning the dog's phobia. The fellow felt sorry for the dog, even thought Samson was cute. Gracie professed herself relieved. "So Samson now lives on a farm. And he's learning to herd sheep!"

That was good for a laugh.

"Who would have thought we would have such international intrigue in our little town?" Abe said. "Personally, I think we can do without any more of it."

"My feelings exactly!" Gracie told him. Rocky just looked at her indulgently.

"Sophie called when she read it in the newspaper. She wanted to make sure I had deadbolt locks. I reminded her this was Willow Bend, for goodness sakes! What a Jewish mother, that woman! 'Never mind,' she says, 'I'll just worry.'"

Gracie furrowed her brow, not getting the reference, and Abe laughed. "You know how many Jewish mothers it takes to change a light bulb?"

Rocky put his palm to his forehead. "I'm sure you're going to tell us even if I don't ask. How many?"

"None," Abe chuckled. "It's all right, I'll sit in the dark."

Rocky groaned. "I'll have the special."

Peach-a-Berry Cobbler

Dough:
- ✓ 1 cup flour
- ✓ 1/2 cup sugar
- ✓ 1-1/2 teaspoons baking powder
- ✓ 1/2 teaspoon salt
- ✓ 1/2 cup milk
- ✓ 1/4 cup butter, softened

Mix all ingredients until smooth.

Fruit:
- ✓ 2 cups sliced peaches
- ✓ 1 cup blueberries (you can use more fruit—Gracie does)
- ✓ 1 tablespoon cornstarch
- ✓ 1 tablespoon butter
- ✓ 1 tablespoon lemon juice
- ✓ 1/4 cup sugar
- ✓ 1/2 cup water or syrup drained from fruit

Combine in large saucepan and cook over low heat until mixture thickens.

Put fruit in 8-inch pan and cover with dough. Sprinkle with 2 tablespoons sugar and 1/4 teaspoon nutmeg. Back at 350 degrees for 30 minutes. Serve warm.

Gracie says, "This is a recipe that Elmo's mother—who was really the mother of my heart, not just a mother-in-law—passed on to me. But she always used more fruit than it calls for, and so do I. I like mixing nectarines with the peaches and black raspberries with the blueberries. It turns a beautiful color that way! (I freeze fresh black raspberries every year when they're in season by laying them out on baking tins and sticking them in the freezer. When the berries are rock-hard, I put them in plastic storage containers and save them for adding to fruit salads, compotes and baked desserts like this one.) Also, I enjoy experimenting with different canned juices to make the liquid for cooking with the fruit. I've found that 1/2 cup of mango or peach juice works very well and adds an extra hint of delicious difference."

About the Author

"I, like Gracie, love homemaking and cooking," writes ROBERTA UPDEGRAFF. "I married my high-school sweetheart, have been married for more than twenty-five years and have three-plus wonderful children. I say plus because our home seems to sprout teenagers and young adults, making our dinner table banter quite lively.

"I am a substitute teacher at Williamsport High School in Pennsylvania, and I love my students! This year I'm teaching drama. I have taught everything from auto mechanics to orchestra. I am also a Sunday school teacher and youth leader. Obviously, I enjoy teenagers.

"Like the Meyers in this story, my husband and I responded to the news reports of Hurricane Mitch, and felt God calling us to offer friendship and labor. We have participated in two work trips to Honduras, and this year we were joined by our youngest daughter and an Italian exchange student. I took puppets and lots of books to work with the children. Next year we're planning to drive a school bus loaded with needed supplies.

"I am a member of the St. David's Christian Writers' Conference board of directors, and I am active in West Branch Christian Writers. Although this is my first book, I have sold numerous articles to publications like *Moody*, *Focus on the Family*, *Group* and *Virtue*."

A NOTE FROM THE EDITORS

This original Guideposts book was created by the Book and Inspirational Media Division of the company that publishes *Guideposts*, a monthly magazine filled with true stories of people's adventures in faith.

Guideposts is available by subscription. All you have to do is write to Guideposts, 39 Seminary Hill Road, Carmel, New York 10512. When you subscribe, each month you can count on receiving exciting new evidence of God's presence, His guidance and His limitless love for all of us.

Guideposts is also available on the Internet by accessing our home page on the World Wide Web at www.guideposts.org. Send prayer requests to our Monday morning Prayer Fellowship. Read stories from recent issues of our magazines, *Guideposts, Angels on Earth, Guideposts for Kids,* and *Guideposts for Teens,* and follow our popular book of devotionals, *Daily Guideposts.* Excerpts from some of our best-selling books are also available.